KAMIKAZE:
THE WIND OF GOD

Bill King

MINERVA PRESS

LONDON

MONTREUX   LOS ANGELES   SYDNEY

KAMIKAZE: THE WIND OF GOD
Copyright © Bill King 1997

ISBN 1 86106 642 2

First Published 1997 by
MINERVA PRESS
195 Knightsbridge
London SW7 1RE

Printed in Great Britain for Minerva Press

KAMIKAZE:
THE WIND OF GOD

OM.

**LEABHARLANNA CHONTAE NA GAILLIMHE
(GALWAY COUNTY LIBRARIES)**

Acc. No. F88,529   Class No. ....

Date of Return	Date of Return	Date of Return

Books are on loan for 21 days from date of issue.

Fines for overdue books: 10p for each week or portion of a week plus cost of postage incurred in recovery.

Author's Preface

Some years after peace broke out in 1945 I formed a strong desire to write an account of the fall of the British Empire

The fall was very personal to me. The immediate cause had been, I considered, the fall of Singapore in 1942 and that had fallen about my ears.

The life style which I had embraced after the war's end, that of an Irish peasant farmer and a single issue organic maniac, left me with no time or opportunity to write and my ambition faded into the background, though not entirely away until I discovered that the subject had been well covered in a brilliant trilogy by James Morris – (*Heaven's Command, Pax Britannica* and *Farewell the Trumpets*) all three books superbly written and painstakingly researched.

A new ambition then rose within me; to write a novel which would encapsulate the fall of the Empire and highlight some of its causes. I had begun to believe that one of the prime reasons for the fall was the failure of the Norman-ruled Anglo-Saxons to relate to the Irish Celts, particularly in the wake of the Reformation Wars between Catholic and Protestants, as a result of which the Britannic Islands were never unified.

Further, I believed that the dismemberment of the Empire was terribly premature. When seeking opinions about the benefits of freedom for the erstwhile British possessions, one cannot consult the millions of men, women and children, who were hacked to death in the aftermath of dissolution, in keeping perhaps with the history of *Homo Sapiens*, which is written in blood.

Most authors' prefaces contain a "without-whose-help-it-would-not" and, yes, I have one.

The late George McBeth, Scottish poet and writer, introduced me to the Hawthornden Castle Writers' Retreat, near Edinburgh, and, there I was fortunate to be granted a fellowship and so this book was written.

A number of friends have greatly aided my efforts with advice and criticism and, if they read this book, they will recognise their contributions and accept my sincere gratitude, which also extends to my publishers, Minerva Press, and to Sioban Piercy who drew the cover.

Contents

Prologue

Modern Hong Kong, a forest of tower blocks thrusting ever closer towards the height of its parent mountain, was, unknowingly, foreshadowed by one of the early spectacular films, "Metropolis", a futuristic conurbation which reduced man to the proportions of an ant. If you now drive through Victoria, the capital of Hong Kong, the concentrated size and power is overwhelming. By half closing and veiling both eyes the megalithic mass can be reduced to a toy town of Lego bricks.

Returning to the remembered experience of Hong Kong in the 1930s is equivalent to peeling off modern London to reveal the ancient Roman town. Hong Kong, built on a bare rock by Scottish merchant adventurers in the early nineteenth century, became frozen in time for a hundred years: a small, pleasantly architected, early Victorian town, fading into Wanchai, the vibrant, crowded Chinese quarter. On a mainland peninsula, north of the busy harbour, the commercial port of Kowloon was dominated by the newly built, grandly pillared Peninsula Hotel (today hardly visible amongst the forest of skyscrapers).

Swinging to the tides in mid-harbour, her anchor cables shackled to a mooring, strongly secured against the devastating recurring typhoons, lay the great, new submarine depot ship, HMS *Medway*, part liner, part floating workshop and storeship.

Secured alongside, on either beam, like a litter of puppies, lay eight or ten newly built fleet submarines, a token counter to the rising threat of Japanese naval power.

At this time war was unthinkable. The flotilla normally lay in Hong Kong enjoying the cool, sunny months of autumn, winter and early spring, at a latitude about fifty miles north of the tropic zone. In May, when the hot, damp south-west monsoon started to blow, the flotilla moved about fifteen hundred miles north to Wei Hai Wei, in Shantung province, where the summer climate was idyllic. Cruises were arranged to Singapore, the Philippines, Borneo, Japan and Manchuria. Time passed pleasantly enough.

The only visible threat was the small but active community of China Coast pirates. The chapter which follows is here described out of context in the timescale of this otherwise consecutive story, which has its origins in an impact of Chinese piracy.

Chapter One

Prelude – The Pirates – Mid 1930s

There is no long, slow, false dawn on the tropical south China Coast; the sun pops up like a jack-in-the-box. The sudden light, bursting in through the square-port window of my austere cabin in the submarine depot ship, woke me as surely as a telephone alarm. As my eyes opened so did the door; Lum Nam, the Chinese "boy", probably aged about forty, padded in, soft-footed, with a cup of hot sweet tea. Somehow he had obtained fresh milk instead of the usual disgusting tinned stuff. I grasped the cup eagerly, propping up on one elbow. "Morning, Lum Nam, what belong?" I enquired routinely.

"Officer go to sea," he replied, laconically, and would go no further, as he bustled around tidying the cabin.

I had not long to wait; in came a signalman, bronzed and beery, holding a message slip. "From your captain, sir," he said and at my bidding read out: "For Lieutenant Howell from commanding officer – the duty destroyer earmarked for anti-piracy patrol has broken down. A submarine is to take her place. The submarine's navigator is sick and the spare crew sub-lieutenant is on leave in Manila. You will deputise for this duty."

I gave a groan. My submarine was refitting in the dockyard; a long refit, which promised to go on for what seemed like forever. I was looking forward to a considerable period to be spent indulging myself in the strenuous activity which suited my personality, mountain climbing, sport and sailing. In addition to that I had a new-found ambition. Brought up in a mixture of strict, middle-class morality, sexual ignorance and naval discipline, I had grown into a monkish and somewhat priggish, perfect, gentle knight. Something in the environment of China and its remoteness from home had released me. I found that I was overwhelmingly interested in the physical aspects of women, though any emotional involvement was stultified. There were tolerated houses in Hong Kong.

The other two men withdrew from the cabin and I sucked away at my tea, ruminating about the coming venture.

Submarines were particularly unsuitable for anti-piracy work. The boats on the China station were designed as fleet submarines, capable of a surface speed of nineteen knots, able to cruise with the fleet or to intercept convoys on the surface in war. Unfortunately, the British were not great at designing diesel engines; at any speed over fourteen knots there would be a thin column of blue smoke from some mechanical disaster. No, what was required was a fast manoeuvrable surface ship, well-gunned, with good boats to lower and plenty of space below for prisoners. Submarines should either kill or be killed.

I had no qualms about navigating the stranger. I had a natural aptitude for coastal pilotage, bearings of prominent objects to clear dangers, the look of a landfall; also I had climbed the mountains surrounding the operating area. Thus, as well as looking down on the charts, I had a mental picture of the lie of the land.

I had a quick shave and cold shower and put on my sea-going uniform. Lum Nam had arranged an early breakfast of bacon, fried bread and eggs, done to my liking, 'over easy' as the Americans call it.

Scrambling onto the bridge of the submarine, I saw that she was ready for sea. I was greeted by the captain, large, ruddy-faced, rough-looking. He was said to be Irish, but had a French sounding name, de something; I suppose descended from a Huguenot nobleman, who had fled the horrors of the religious wars in France. A Protestant seeking sanctuary in Catholic Ireland. "Good morning, pilot," he said and detailed the situation between draughts from an enormous mug of coffee, which gave off a vile aroma, emphasising the fact that, in those days, the British usually preferred tea. He continued:

"We have to patrol off Chilang point, a long, low peninsula sticking out into the sea to the north of us. There is a lighthouse on the end of it manned by a retired naval rating. They say that he is a bit eccentric and has one or two Chinese wives, but he cannot desert as it's too far to walk. The first lieutenant has put out the charts and navigational gear; no doubt you can find your way and, for good measure, you can take the ship out of the harbour. I will be sitting around in case you are in trouble." He then retired under the bridge cab roof with his odious coffee.

I had no difficulty in detaching the submarine from the depot ship, but my heart was in my mouth as we wove through the teeming traffic in the harbour. Junks, sampans, ferries and small motorboats crisscrossed and played "last across" with scant appreciation of danger. This was excellent training for me and I felt grateful that the skipper's ancestors had not been skewered in the "night of the long knives", the massacre of the French Protestants in Paris.

Finally, we shook clear of the narrow waters of the harbour's exit at Lye Mun and set a course to pass Chilang Lighthouse. I relaxed and had a look at the local orders.

As usual, whatever you did in this situation was wrong; either you were reprimanded for being pusillanimous or, if too audacious, prosecuted as a criminal. Of course, no one studied the intricacies of international law, but there were some broad rules for inducing a suspicious vessel to heave to for visit and search.

1. Make a signal in international code "Heave to or I fire".
2. If this is ignored, fire a shot across her bows.
3. If this indication is ignored, fire a round *into* her bows.

I think it had to be solid shot and not explosive. Perhaps you could follow up with explosive, if this was ignored. Even in war, submarines were supposed to succour survivors; this of course, they could not possibly do, in their overcrowded interiors, particularly if ruthless people were among them. Certainly the Chinese pirates topped the bill for merciless behaviour.

We slipped into a routine; the crew in three watches, patrolling just north of the Chilang peninsula, the radio operator listening on the merchant vessels' distress frequency. I kept track of the navigation and radio signals and stood watch. The other officers were bar-room acquaintances in the depot ship but submarine crews are a close-knit group and it was like being in a foreign country.

I remembered that the wardroom Chinese cook, Yin Dong, was renowned for his expertise and I looked forward to meals at which the uninteresting naval rations would be transformed by the art of a master.

There followed days and nights of fruitless endeavour performing a square dance around the probable route of pirated ships. The pirates' technique was to board the ships at their departure ports, disguised as passengers, with weapons concealed or somehow smuggled aboard. On a dark night, they would erupt with terrifying violence, slaughtering or overpowering the guards and crew, then forcing the captain to take the ship into their lair at Bias Bay, in Chinese territory, just north of Hong Kong. China, at that time, had been carved up by a number of rival war lords. There was no effective central government and precious little law and order.

We had been on patrol for about three days. I was sitting in the wardroom having lunch with the first lieutenant and engineer officer. Physically, the first lieutenant resembled a smaller edition of his captain. He was didactic and loquacious, the warrant engineer officer small, silent and withdrawn. They are now shadowy figures and I forget their names. We were eating a ragout of tinned meat and vegetables, which was normally repellent. Yin Dong had transformed it with spices, ground herbs and little slices of ginger, and it was a pleasant meal with a background orchestration of hammering diesel engines and the roar of overhead fans ventilating the dangerous, explosive gas which rose from the huge electric batteries now being recharged beneath our feet. I was happy to sit masticating and listening to the first lieutenant's monologue.

"This is the God-damn stupidest operation in history! Can you imagine going alongside a merchant ship with our paper-thin saddle tanks? How are we to board with our flimsy canvas boat in anything more than flat calm, damn it, if I am to lead the attack, I should practise holding a cutlass in my teeth. These pirates are absolute bastards; they hold wealthy Chinese to ransom, cut bits off them and post the bits to their relatives; sell pretty girls into harems; no one controls them; they pay 'cum shaw' to the local warlord and – " At that moment, there was a metallic cry from the Tannoy internal broadcasting system – "gun action stations."

Reluctantly, dropping my knife and fork, I raced for the bridge, pushing past hurrying figures in the narrow corridor leading to the control room and bridge ladder. The engine room telegraphs clanged to "full ahead" and there was an increased roar from the engines.

I shot up the vertical, conning tower brass ladder, as the submarine heeled slightly under full rudder. The captain was conning the ship to pass close off Chilang Lighthouse to the south of us. "Take over pilot," he said and then detailed the situation. "The lighthouse keeper remembered his Morse code and flashed a signal to us – a ship is acting suspiciously out of sight behind the peninsula, probably pirated. They have obviously clobbered the radio operator and will aim for Bias Bay, as soon as they have full control; we may just catch them, we have revolutions for fourteen knots." As I ducked under the bridge cab roof, to work at the chart table, I heard the crash of the gun tower hatches opening just forward of the bridge. The gun's crew were erupting onto the gun platform and there was a crisp order, "Load with a practice round, hand up high explosive." The Captain turned to his second in command, the first lieutenant, "As soon as we are in the lee of the land you can unstow the Berthon boat." This was a folding dinghy, lashed down inside the light metal casings, which made a deck over the strong, whale-shaped pressure hull of the submarine. The first lieutenant was mustering a crew of two armed toughs and he carried a .45" Webley and Scott revolver in a holster; it had done service in the 1914 war and there were some mysterious notches in the handle.

As we thundered round Chilang point, a small passenger cum cargo vessel came into sight, stern on, gathering speed and heading for Bias Bay.

The signalman was flashing the general international call sign and, at our inadequate signal mast, flew code flags indicating "Heave to or I fire." There was no response from the miscreants and the vessel continued on her way. I was busy plotting positions and courses and gauging our relative speeds; we had the legs of her, and we would catch her, just.

The chase continued and, as we drew close, I could see the situation on deck. A band of ruffians, armed with guns and staves, were herding the terrified passengers, separating obviously well-to-do folk and young women from the amorphous crowd of blue-trousered peasantry.

We drew up on the windward quarter of the fleeing ship, so that smoke would move away from us. There was still no response from the fugitive nor slackening of speed. There was a pause, which, in the fraught circumstances, seemed endless. Then the captain said calmly, "Fire a shot across her bows." There was a jarring bang and almost instantaneously, a green and white plume rose from the sea ahead of the undeviating vessel. Again there was a pause, the silence broken by the continuous clicking of the signal lamp. Scarcely raising his voice the captain said, "Fire a round into her fore peak." The shell hit fair and square about six feet above the water line. There was a violent explosion; someone had loaded a high explosive round in error and a fire was breaking out in the fore peak of our victim, which continued at unslackened speed towards Bias Bay. I trained my binoculars on her bridge; a man dressed like a Chinese farmer was holding a pistol to the captain's head. The ship turned for the pirates' hide-out, where a fleet of junks and sampans were jilling around the offing, inside Chinese territorial waters. Our captain, with no emotion nor rising tone, ordered, "Break off the action. Number One find out why they loaded high explosives." And to me "Pilot, draft out a signal to the Commodore Hong Kong."

In the wash-up our captain was sued by the owners of the vessel for a sum of two million pounds, the price of replacing the vessel, and was then tactfully appointed elsewhere out of the jurisdiction of the local courts. I absorbed some useful lessons about life in the raw.

This local happening loomed very large for me, brisked me up as a warlike person, held in the timewarp of a deceptive peace, which could flare into war as a result of some incident which could appear trivial, such as the act of an over-zealous or over-excited seaman loading a round of live shot. In 1931 some politician decided to cut the already abysmal pay of naval ratings. The British Home Fleet, stationed at Invergordon in Scotland, broke out in open mutiny. Ten days later the Japanese invaded Manchuria, the foundations of World War II were laid.

Chapter Two

Introduction

The past, particularly the recent past, is well documented. The truth of the documentation is much distorted by prejudice; conclusions and opinions are frequently warped by hindsight. The present, thanks to the invention of very sophisticated equipment, is portrayed with an appalling clarity. There used to be a saying of the Russian peasants, which assured them a comfortable anonymity, "Heaven is high and the Tsar is far away." Now nothing is further away than the nearest television set.

We appear to live in a linear space-time warp, though modern scientists tell us that this is not so. The future is not ours to see. Nevertheless, precognition, thought transference and extrasensory perception are already on the drawing board. There is, maybe, a destiny, which shapes our ends, rough-hew them how we will; conversely, our fates may lie not in our stars but in ourselves.

These random thoughts bear on what I am about to recount, which concerns the crashing of far-flung empires, entwined with the fate lines of individuals, some of them riding the tigers, which are impossible to dismount, the tigers of frightful power.

My background is here very briefly described, so you may understand, perhaps with sympathy, the unfolding of this bizarre tale.

My parents died in India when I, an only child, was very young. Father was serving with his regiment. He volunteered to drive a relief train into an area where there was a cholera epidemic. He contracted terminal cholera. This broke my mother's heart and will to live. I was brought up by a stiff-necked, childless aunt, in upper middle-class circumstances, in Yorkshire. She had inherited an enormous fortune from a ship-owning grandfather but left none of it to me. She distrusted my youthful indiscipline. I now think that her decision was correct and based on adequate causes. She sent me to the Royal Naval

College Dartmouth as an embryo naval officer at the age of thirteen, partly to make a man of me and partly to resuscitate the image of her husband, who had been killed at the Battle of Jutland. My aunt used to frighten me with the doctrine of everlasting hellfire; even now I can hardly enjoy a barbecue.

I started badly at the Naval College, not being good at rugby football and unused to the company of other boys and men. I was much teased about my poor physique and then obstinately set myself to master gymnastics, finally becoming the foremost schoolboy gymnast of the year. This sport carried no cachet, at that time, but the unedifying post of a gentleman circus performer enabled me to work off some of the devilment, which had so annoyed my aunt. This was the springtime of my life.

Now, in my winter, I live near the small port of Soller, in Majorca, a Spanish island in the Western Mediterranean.

I have an undefined illness which has resulted from lack of oxygen and a surfeit of carbon dioxide during many years of submarine warfare. Doctors cannot name it, as they have not seen anyone else, who has had a similar environment, for so long. In addition, what is lacking in my medical history sheet is the emotional blow, which I will recount and which took from me the desire to live and robbed me of the strength to die.

I draw a small pension, which was designed to keep retired officers in fallen gentry conditions; but the value of the money has diminished. I consider this to be a blessing to me. If I had drawn a living wage, I might have tried to achieve some sort of middle-class existence, perhaps even to marry. Both these states would be impossible to someone who has experienced an emotional death.

I rent two little huts on the mountainside, one high up in the terraces among the olive trees, the other down near the sea in the shade of a bamboo grove. I alternate between the huts according to the season. This is the only climate in which I could exist.

I have enough money to live on the sparse but excellent food of the Majorcan peasant without the hard toil, which is not possible for me. I remain a healthy invalid and do what is within my power to help my neighbours with their chores.

When the breeze stirs the leaves of the olive trees, I lie in their dappled shade. When the temporales, blow I come inside and light a fire of twigs and fir cones.

Happiness is a relative state.

One prisoner of war of the Japanese was flogged to death with a wire whip but failed to die. A great many Christians believe that this sort of fate awaits all sinners for eternity.

Happiness is the reverse of despair; the ability not to feel sorry for oneself. The philosopher Jung postulated that ninety per cent of people would be happier if they were Catholics. Many northern Protestants and their semi-heathen peripheral fringe busy themselves with a dutiful, functional justification. Judging from the Latin tag "labore est orare" – "to work is to pray", the Romans must have been incipient Protestants.

I cannot climb any of these ladders, I look for a way. Right now my way is very slowly up a straggly path through the early-ripening spring crops. I stop at the end of a terrace and breathe the air of the sea breeze. It is free.

Chapter Three
Malta – Late 1920s

The door burst open. Three young men, with the immaturity of a close-knit group apparent in their movement, flung themselves into an empty room. The gun room, a word which once described the repository for squires' fowling pieces, was the junior officers' quarters in a great, lumbering battleship of the British Mediterranean Fleet. Normally overcrowded and noisy, the room was now deserted, its emptiness obscene, the bare, white-painted steel walls and square-port windows a harsh backdrop. Outside, in the harbour, the relentless summer sun hit the array of great, floating metal boxes forming the cutting edge of British sea power, which exercised dominion over palm and pine; our navies had not yet melted away.

In this small space, hard by the guns, we were housed in crowded disorder, the young officers, cadets, midshipmen and sub-lieutenants, who were later to take the fleet and its aircraft to war. Some would rise to rank or fame; many would have no other grave but the sea. Those who were left would witness the sunset of an Empire, which had been like a great wave rising to its zenith at Queen Victoria's Jubilee in 1887 and then, like a swell whose rotating base catches the sea bottom, it steepened, became fragile and finally broke on the shore.

Unheeding the wider scene, we burst into our deserted home, glad to be on our own, three eager fledgling officers; all the others had gone away, rifle shooting or something. A sleepy Maltese steward was roused to supply mugs of tea and we sat down around the scarred, wooden table.

In retrospect, I now think that this was the moment when a long, slow process crystallised and a firm, lasting friendship was forged between three very disparate young men. Apart from ordinary differences of character, we bestrode the British class system; at that time fixed by taboos even more rigid than racial barriers.

I can see myself as I was then, dimly through the mists of time; Saxon, fair and beefy, middle-class and somewhat stupid, not so much academically as through lacking an enquiring mind and soon to be enthralled by obsessive heterosexual desires, a state which dulls the brain. I had immense good fortune to be admitted into close friendship with two men, whom I regarded then, and still regard, in retrospect, as superior beings.

The elder was Simon Dunbulben the only son of the Earl of Mountbriach, a shadowy Irish figure of whom I knew nothing.

Simon's general appearance at the time is best described in French – *joli laid*. I suppose the English equivalent is "agreeably ugly". His craggy, bowed, high-coloured Norman Irish face was already forming out of the puppy fat of youth. His expression was dominated by quick intelligence and the air of absolute authority born of many hundreds of years of squirearchal rule. All this gave him a total lack of self-consciousness or embarrassment. He was naturally gravitating towards the branch of the Navy which dealt with communication, then mostly the preserve of the upper class. Admirals needed their flag lieutenants, the naval equivalent of the military ADC, to be socially apt and poised.

Tom Farr was an exception. His father came from a long line of Norfolk peasants and was gamekeeper to a nobleman with great wealth, lands and splendid pheasant coverts. The gamekeeper had married a pretty schoolteacher, delicate but very bright of mind. Doubtless at his wife's behest, the gamekeeper, with the authority of an old servant, had persuaded his noble employer that the gamekeeper's only son, educated primarily by his mother, should be sent to the Royal Naval College Dartmouth and obtain a commission in the Royal Navy. There was, of course, some difficulty with the Admiralty Selection Board members, who were at that time watchdogs against this sort of infiltration. Nonetheless, the noble squire had the ear of the monarch, who liked to shoot pheasants, and Tom, his country burr ironed out by his mother, went, accordingly to Dartmouth. Tom was exceptionally bright. He had probably the best brain in the Navy and not only of his own generation. His rightful destiny should have led him to the top of his profession. He had inherited splendid country-bred good looks, which had been hollowed out by his mother's fragility.

So, how did I fit in and why? Only I think because we all shared a very lively sense of humour, a disregard for pomposity and the fact that I was prepared to subordinate my lesser intelligence without resentment.

So much for intelligence. What of character? Tom was a nice person; he did not have to try to be nice, he just was. Simon was moderately nice, most people are. I was not nice, not nice at all; not so much because I sought power or gain but because I did not have love.

Simon was homosexual. I was, perhaps, almost the only person in the Navy who knew this. He explained it to me without embarrassment because he wished to make it clear that our friendship existed without sexual impact. "You are not my type," he said, without a trace of unease. He explained to me the two main types of homosexuality. One the genetic, immutable imprint which was his; the other, the induced kind, found among mostly military, sporting men, men without women, single-sex schools, prisons, lunatic asylums and fantasies. Simon also told me that he was in complete control, would never make a fool of himself in the fleet and rejected sodomy, which is by no means confined to homosexuals. I wondered if Simon had explained his homosexuality to Tom and then thought, "No, he probably thought Tom was bright enough to cotton on."

We sat now at the table, drawing at the warm, sweet tea, glad of the unaccustomed quiet and privacy, continuing some debate.

"The human situation," said Tom, "consists mainly of the difference between men and women and their antithetic desires. The woman wants care and loving, children or family, above all security; men just want to have it off."

I rose to the bait. "What, are there no whores, nymphomaniacs or bitches? Do women have no arousals or orgasms? Are they all Virgin Marys?"

Simon intervened quietly, "Tom was speaking in general terms, Bob; he has a good point and also, if this sort of thing was explained to everyone at puberty, they would have a far better chance of contentment."

"Well," I grumbled, "don't men fall in love, what about chivalry?"

Tom rejoined, "In chivalry there are few Sir Galahads but many Sir Lancelots."

"Yes," I remembered, "he was the chap who screwed the queen."

There was a torrent of noise and the rest of the gun room inhabitants poured in through the door, dusty, sunburned and thirsty, boasting of their scores at shooting. One had been on duty at the butts and said quietly to me, "I heard all those bullets whistling above me and thought what it must have been like in the bullet stream in the trenches in Flanders. Each bullet is determined to make a hole in your guts."

But for now there was to be no war, not for another ten years, a prophetic span which never diminished.

Everyone was clamouring for tea, the stewards protesting; one of the returned shooters, resenting our enclosed friendship, sneered, "Ah, the three classes. The upper class is cruel, arrogant and exclusive; the middle class envious, insecure and litigious; the lower class, noisy, violent and beery."

"Yes," replied Tom, "but we are moving towards a classless society which will combine all those qualities."

Chapter Four
Malta – Late 1920s: A Paper Chase

Girt around by the mightiest fortress of medieval Christendom, our battle fleet lay in peaceful harmony; the most powerful fighting force in the world, forming the teeth of the British Empire which spanned the globe; the one in the schoolroom with huge areas of red and a multitude of little red dots indicating strategic island bases. Pax Britannica was established. There could not, there must not, be a war, well not for at least ten years.

The ships lay, hove up tight, between the mooring buoys, the nuzzles of the great guns burnished to mirror brightness, the vast teak decks scrubbed white as hounds' teeth. Enamelled paintwork reflected the harsh sunlight, rows of sailors lined the decks, their spotless, white uniforms creating an impression of cleanliness which could only be surpassed by heavenly choirs. It was Sunday, the time of divisional inspection and church parade. I was midshipman of the watch, assisted by cadet Tom Farr, my junior by twelve months. A moderate breeze off the land brought the smells of a city, still medieval in its sanitation, and kicked up the harbour into little wavelets. The brightly painted dghaisas, the local rowing taxi boats, danced in the poppling water and the sun reflected off their kaleidoscopic decorations; their sturdy sun-browned rowers stood to the oars keeping the boats, grouped round each huge warship, from being blown into a confused melee. Tom and I, dressed in our best white uniforms, buttoned up to the neck, the laundry rust marks carefully camouflaged with white chalk, paced up and down the quarterdeck. Telescopes, under each of our left arms, were held horizontal by some agonised, secret muscles in the armpit. We walked in step, turning inwards towards each other at the end of our beat and awaited the unfolding of the next act in our pageant.

The officer of the watch, (I forget his name but remember that he was a rugby football international of whom we were in considerable awe), let out a crisp command and we ceased our perambulations and stationed ourselves where we could see both the flagship, about two hundred yards north of us, and also the King's Stairs, a landing jetty at the foot of the great, fortified city of Valetta. Here, bobbing in the choppy water, skilfully fended off by her picked crew, lay the "Green Parrot". She was a steam pinnace, the Commander-in-Chief's "barge", though anything less like a barge one could scarcely imagine. Resembling an old-fashioned steam yacht, she gleamed from bow to stern; the brass funnel shone like gold. The cabin and stern sheets were embellished with all manner of marine handicraft. The green, enamel-painted hull bore not a single blemish or brush mark. I focused my telescope on her, remarking to Tom, "God, she is like a jewel, emerald and gold" but was interrupted by someone descending our quarterdeck ladder, like a cascade, and speeding across the deck. Simon, Midshipman Viscount Dunbulben, assistant to our signal officer, came to a halt in front of the officer of the watch, saluted and said, "Signal from the flagship, sir, C in C will be afloat with flag flying at 0900." Simon had barely turned to go before the order "Pipe the guard and band" passed down our hierarchy to be executed by the trill of the boatswain's mate's whistle followed by his cry, somewhat hoarse from Saturday night's beer. A bugle call rang out; in no time the immaculate Royal Marines were in line, with bayonets fixed. All had grooved into place as a flurry of activity agitated the area around the King's Stairs.

Through my telescope I could see the magnificent figure of the admiral stepping aboard his barge. One could scarcely believe that mortal man could be so superb, looking like some actor, perfectly cast for the part. Bred from an immensely long line of landowning noblemen, whose younger sons had served in the armed services or colonial government, his handsome face and complexion radiated self-confidence, health and unquestioned authority. The barge sped off towards the flagship, the dghaisas scattering like a flock of brightly coloured birds.

As the barge neared us and turned to spread the ceremonial of its passage over us, at a nod from the officer of the watch, I gave the order; the Royal Marine bugler, matching the occasion with his art, blew the seven dancing notes of the "alert", the boatswain's mate's pipes shrilled, nine hundred men on the upper deck sprang to attention; the rifles of the Royal Marine Guard crashed in the "General Salute"; the bandmaster poised for a second and then burst forth with the Commander-in-Chief's salute. It was the chorus of that stirring ditty "Rule Britannia". The melody suited the occasion; the barge passed, flying the undefaced red cross of St George on a white background which fluttered stiffly like silk – it was silk! The admiral passed on to his flagship, acknowledging our salute and mounted his gangway to receive full honours from a galaxy of talent and smartness on the quarterdeck.

Our ship returned to normal and the inspections prior to church were completed. The sun shone from cloudless blue and under the huge awning and in the breeze it was pleasantly cool. With my telescope I examined the great fortress of honey-coloured stone rising above and around us. It never failed to please me with a feeling of reassurance. Here we were in the centre of the great fleet, which could, at a few hours' notice, steam either homewards to protect our country or eastwards along a chain of supporting bases to where the vast army of India could be transported to any trouble spot. But there were no trouble spots now.

I think Tom heard it first for he looked rapidly in all directions. A high-pitched, droning sound was increasing. "Look up sun," said Tom, shielding his eyes with his fingers. A black dot was coming out of the glare.

"Holy Moses," I said, "it's a fighter aircraft. What on earth is he doing airborne on a Sunday?"

Simon had now rejoined us on the quarterdeck, also goggling at the fast approaching machine. He just had time to say "there have been no signals about an exercise" when things began to happen fast. The drone rose to a roar. The plane flattened out, skimming across the harbour. I just had time to identify her as a Fleet Air Arm fighter, but with some strange container fixed in her underbelly. The plane came straight for the flagship, then swerved upwind of her. I could see the pilot's form in the cockpit. Just before the plane crossed the bow of the flagship, there was a movement in the bubble-like container and a fluttering snowstorm descended; no, it was a stained snowstorm; the flakes were brown, like autumn leaves; the whole ship was carpeted from stern to stern. As the plane jerked upwards to clear the fortress, Simon swung his telescope onto the flagship, focusing very carefully. "Good God," he said "it's bumph." The flagship was covered with myriads of sheets of that brown, cheap, crinkly stuff which the Admiralty issued as lavatory paper.

Tom said softly, "I think I will opt for the submarine service."

I muttered, "It could not happen in war; all these anti-aircraft guns."

Simon said, "Well there will be one less pilot in the Fleet Air Arm, tomorrow, but he made his point."

Many of the brown leaves blew listlessly into the sea to be finally dissolved.

Chapter Five
Gibraltar – Late 1920s

In springtime, the Mediterranean fleet steamed to its western border; the Home fleet ventured southward. The whole might of the British Navy assembled at Gibraltar.

The Rock, in silhouette a huge crouching lion, taken from Spain, looks out across the narrow straits towards its complement, Ceuta, filched by Spain from Africa. In between, the water is pushed into the evaporating Mediterranean by the prevailing westerly wind but this piles up too much water inside, so a counter current runs outward ninety feet down, which is useful for submarines or tuna fish wishing to enter or leave through the straits. They select the depth where the current is favourable.

Tom Farr and I, our ship temporarily housing an admiral, enjoyed a berth alongside the jetty and had wangled a day's leave to climb the Rock, taking with us a picnic lunch, sandwiches, disgusting to anyone of sophisticated taste, sheets of white bread and bully beef. I had a single chocolate bar. I was looking forward to the chance to stretch my legs and listen to the outpourings of Tom's fertile, enquiring mind.

We were wearing sportsgear, shirts and shorts but, being clearly recognised as officers were treated to a smart salute at the dockyard gates which we returned by doffing our hats; they were trilbies which you seldom see nowadays.

We wandered down the main street of the little town, noisy, smelly, busy, cheerful, mostly Spanish, part British, part African; the local mercantile hierarchy was Genoese. Everyone was swarthy or sun-bronzed. None of the merchandise, carpets, beads or whatnots, noisily offered for sale, held the slightest interest for us, nor if they had could we have afforded to buy any of them. We turned to climb one of the narrow, ascending streets, free of wheeled traffic being a series of stone steps which finally gave out onto the zigzag of ramps and paths leading to the summit ridge, from whence the Rock dropped away, wedge-shaped and steep, to the sea on either side. As we swung easily up the steps of the street, bordered by small dwelling houses, a door opened on my right; a young girl, aged about twenty, carrying a basket on her hip, stepped out and paused, staring at the strangers. I was aware of the roundness of her cheeks, eyes, breasts and bottom, of dark ringleted curls, of all the fire of Spain and Africa. I had difficulty in swallowing and I think that a lot of my subsequent troubles stemmed from that moment of delayed sexual awakening. We climbed on.

I heard Tom give a chuckle, "I thought your eyes were going to pop out."

The town thinned out and then suddenly died. Our route went over the bluff at the north end of the Rock, which overlooked a flat piece of no-man's-land and the Spanish border. We came to an army checkpoint guarding the military installations along the crest of the great fortress. A magnificent corporal, kilted in a Seaforth tartan, demanded our identity cards and then saluted smartly – "pass, sor." We had nearly reached the crest-walk, which doubles back towards the south. Out to seaward, the westerly wind, funnelling in through the straits, was breaking the crests of the swells. Gibraltar Bay is well sheltered by the Spanish hills. Down in the harbour it was calm; up on the ridge there was a cooling light wind. We sat on a ledge of rock to eat our sandwich lunch and contemplate the spectacular panorama below us. To the east, the concrete-covered rock plunged steeply down into a huge water catchment; if this failed to supply the colony, water had to be brought in by tankers. On the other side the harbour and bay were carpeted by warships. How could those navies ever melt away?

A small tribe of Barbary apes were going about their business in the bushes just below us, hoping for scraps from our lunch. We munched silently for a short time. I said to Tom, "So what about sex?" impelled by the recent, brief encounter in the town.

"Fun," he replied. I could see that his attention was on the apes.

"How do you know?"

"I've read the manuals, pornography and romance; I have imagination."

"Have you masturbated?"

Tom gave a laugh. "Of course I have, everyone has – it's exploratory." He looked curiously at my expression. "Great Scott, Bob, you don't, never have."

I stammered foolishly, aghast at his perception, "I thought it was wrong – my aunt – "

"Well your sainted aunt, anyhow the real thing is not within my financial horizon; wife, mistress, casual affair, cheap trollops, it all costs money."

Tom chucked a crust to the eager apes below and started another sandwich. I noticed that he had no chocolate bar; it would have cost two pence. Then I remembered that his father, the gamekeeper, had been killed in a shooting accident, his noble employer, purple-faced from vintage port, had blown some fuse in his heart. Tom's mother kept her cottage and had a small stipend from the estate (which also paid for Tom's naval uniform and plain clothes). She was too frail to work. Tom remitted a portion of his minute pay to help with her upkeep; he would remain virginal for a very long time. I broke off half my chocolate bar and pressed it on him. Tom chewed the half bar, gratefully. It put him in a didactic mood and without my questioning or prompting he remarked:

"There are five ways in which sex goes wrong, only five: broken hearts, broken homes, unwanted children, harmful perversions and venereal disease."

"And the harmful perversions?"

"Again five." Tom held up five fingers. "Sadistic cruelty, child abuse, rape, buggery and bestiality."

"So you think homosexuality is a harmful perversion?"

"I did not say that." Tom rose; we brushed off the crumbs and threw two more crusts to the apes capering about with their young, the legendary guardians of British rule on the Rock.

We resumed our walk along the crest. On our right hand lay the town, dockyard and, beyond that, the harbour, the bay and the mighty fleet.

I determined to continue probing Tom. "Look at that great steel city in the water below us. Here we are in the command echelon of the real might of this vast empire, which daubs and flecks the map with red."

Tom considered, while we climbed a small rise in the ridge, "It's obsolete, some of these ships were for Jutland but they didn't do very well there. The British people lost their faith in sea power; Gallipoli and Jutland should have been like Copenhagen and Trafalgar; Nelson was on his column. The 1921 naval treaty laid down a ratio of naval power 5.5.3 for Britain, the USA and Japan. Japan lost face and became bitter; the USA doesn't need a big navy at present; the far-flung British overseas Empire does."

I looked down into the bay again. "But those two new battleships, Rodney and Nelson, 16 inch guns and great armoured boxes." Again there was a pause for thought. Tom halted and looked down on the fleet.

"To be effective in interception and action a battleship must be capable of thirty knots; those do twenty-three with luck. To drive a huge, armoured battery at speed you need very powerful engines and the maximum speed of a floating body is governed by its waterline length; that is an immutable law of hydro-dynamics. To defeat the law you must either skim the surface or go beneath it and part the water."

This was beyond my scientific comprehension but I pointed out the battlecruiser, HMS *Hood*, "Plenty of waterline length and speed there."

"Yes," said Tom, "the Germans built armoured honeycombs; that ship is a lightly protected pleasure craft."

"Oh, balls," I said, "you are exaggerating."

Tom replied, "If anyone built a sixty thousand ton ship, these would all be obsolete."

"Well," I was building up resentment, "there are four aircraft carriers with the two fleets."

Tom did not pause. "The aircraft are RAF rejects, the pilots mostly RAF. The RAF controls Coastal Command and the balance of carriers to battleships is not enough, the carrier is now the capital ship."

I had enough of Tom's iconoclasm and dropped the subject. We walked on, looking mostly to the eastward, where the blue Mediterranean stretched to the horizon. About a mile out of the lee of the rock a few small fishing boats bobbed in the little waves, the westerly wind curling up to the northward, driving the cold Atlantic water towards the hot beaches of eastern Spain. As we continued southward along the ridge, I determined to make another foray.

"Tom, what about religion? Do you think there is anything beyond Sunday divisions and church on the quarterdeck?"

Tom paused and turned towards the East, gripping the iron handrail which prevented us from failing onto the concrete catchment and cascading into the catchwater a thousand feet below us.

"Yes, I am a Christian believer without faith; I have come to believe in a universal religion entirely intellectually."

He paused and scratched his head. I had got to know Tom's head scratches; if you asked a wet question, he scratched the back of his head and if the question merited consideration he scratched his forehead. This was a frontal scratch.

"Deep thought is burdensome, so when scientists expanded the frontiers of human knowledge, they rejected God because of the archaism of religious teaching. They overlooked the fact that it was written as an allegory for primitive people. The clerics responded by proscribing scientific advance. There are still flat-earthers around. If you contemplate the huge spread of the macrocosm, the galactic universe, the infinitesimal measure of the atomic microcosm, all these molecules have not come together by chance; there is obviously a plan, there must be a planner."

I broke in, "What sort of planner?"

"Observing that loving behaviour very frequently engenders happiness the planner must love; Christianity measures up to all this."

As Tom was becoming unsure, I thought I might trump his ace.

"Well Tom, why do you think God sent his Son down here at that particular time and place?"

There was another head scratch.

"It is not possible to teach a coherent religion, based on love, to a vast crowd of uneducated, warring tribesmen. Palestine, in the year zero, was the meeting place of the spiritual discipline of Judaic Monotheism – the mental discipline of the Greek philosophers and the political discipline of the Roman Empire."

I took some time to absorb this before making a lame and not too nice rejoinder.

"Very good thinking, Tom, but, maybe, the Virgin Mary was the only woman ever to be without sin."

He paused silent and brooding. "Does this sound pompous to you, Bob? Descartes had words for it, 'I think, therefore I am'."

Silence fell on us as we enjoyed the view and vast expanse, which had rewarded our climb. I considered Tom's insight into the world of adult, sexual turmoil from which I had been largely protected by a blanket of withheld information, black threats of retribution and a disciplined poverty. For me, the connection between the salacious contents of dirty books, furtively read and passed around, and the high ideals of exclusive love between man and woman was still hidden.

Tom having been through Dartmouth from the age of thirteen to seventeen, simultaneously cramming a secondary and a naval education, was, like the rest of us, not scholastically educated. I knew that he read widely and avidly, absorptive as a sponge, and that his fertile, enquiring mind left nothing uncritically considered.

He finished, "There is more cruelty and bullshit woven into religion than into any other subject."

We dropped down the descending slope of the ridge to the southward, towards the naval hospital and the town, where the streets wound back towards the dockyard gate giving towards the mole where our ship was berthed. I sensed that Tom had had enough of my questioning but could not forbear to pursue further, "Eternity, Tom, heaven or hell, it's a long time – too long."

Tom stopped to re-tie a shoe lace and straightened up with a dismissive air, "I don't think time is linear." He was silent for a dozen steps. "Probably cyclical, perhaps helical or circular."

A taxi roared past us, the driver thumping the door of the car with his arm, the only permitted warning in Gibraltar. We were soon back to the line of great ships, their guns at rest like couched lances.

Shortly after these incidents and conversations, Tom and I decided that we would join the Submarine Service. There followed a long period of training and apprenticeship, which does not merit detail but which led me, by stages, to the post of second-in-command of one His Majesty's submarines. Under the eye of an experienced commanding officer, I would have to run the ship effectively or get out. There was, however, one meaningful interlude.

Chapter Six
1929 – It would have been so easy

We climbed quickly up the low cliffs, little more than high sand dunes, and then over a gentle slope, across parched tussocks to the crest of the ridge.   On our right, the straight sea-path of the Dardanelles pointed into the Sea of Marmara, the Bosporus, the Black Sea and towards the heart of Asia.

I was treasuring the brief re-encounter with Tom and Simon, now a communications officer on the chief's staff.   A small Naval squadron was visiting Constantinople for a tour of reconciliation. Eight years previously, Mustafa Kemal (now styled Kemal Atatürk) had defied and ejected the occupying allies in spite of their victory in 1918.   After the Sultan had been deposed, he forged Turkey into a powerful, secular state.   Now it was time to extend a friendly hand, currently represented by two battleships (one the Mediterranean Fleet flagship) in peaceful array and accompanied by two destroyers.

Tom and I, both serving in submarine appointments, had been temporarily drafted to one of the destroyers.   I think that the idea behind our inclusion was a nostalgic desire of some veteran staff officer to pay a tribute to those submariners who had played a valiant part in the abortive attempt to force the passage to Constantinople in 1915.   However, we kept our submarine connection low-keyed during this diplomatic situation and concentrated on shaking the hands of our erstwhile enemies.

The squadron was now anchored bow and stern, close by the Dolmar Bagtche, the one-time palace of the Sultan and now a museum.   Our destroyer had been detached to anchor off the Gallipoli beaches at the entry into the Dardanelles from the Mediterranean.   A small party had been landed for a sightseeing picnic, right where our forces had made a humiliating withdrawal in January 1916 after suffering frightful casualties.   At least the blood had washed away, if not the memories. Was this sort of rubbing our noses in it to appease our Turkish friends?

The rest of the party were having a swim or lolling around on the beach. We three walked up and along the ridge, and to my amazement, we came upon a battlefield left uncleared after fourteen years. The dead men had been removed but there were horses' skeletons, shell craters and empty food tins lying in haphazard disarray.

"They must have been too busy with other matters," said Tom. Simon kicked aside a rusty bully beef tin. "Or, perhaps, it's a good idea for a war memorial, less pompous than the usual thing and totally representational."

"One of my uncles was killed here." I said this for effect. Actually, he had been killed at Kat-el-Amara, in Mesopotamia. "They never found his body; we might have a look around here." Getting no response, I went on, "Why did we have to lose? Was the strategy faulty?"

Simon dived straight in. "No, the grand strategy was sound; to outflank the Central European enemies and link up with our shaky Russian allies..."

Tom interrupted, "It failed twice, the first naval assault because Nelson was on his column." He paused knowing that it took me a while to catch up with his flights of fancy.

"Yes," I followed on, "if Nelson had been in command, the fleet would have forced the Dardanelles like at Copenhagen. The Sultan was preparing to flee."

Then I recalled but did not mention the fact that Nelson had subsequently entered the Baltic and dissuaded the Russians from joining Napoleon in a Confederacy of the North. He turned the other flank of Europe.

Tom broke into my reverie, "The British Fleet was stopped by a small minefield laid from a caique by a Turkish Lieutenant-Commander, just there." He pointed across the Straits and continued, "The second, long-winded, military assault failed because the Turks, with the help of German military engineering expertise, had time to fortify the Peninsula. Most of our commanders were those who could best be spared from the Western Front and the seas to the westward of it."

I then recalled a recent conversation with a Turkish officer, who had actually been there. He spoke good English in dramatic fashion.

"We were being bombarded by a British battleship one afternoon. We were fighting back with our coast defence guns; our ammunition supply was running low; defeat stared us in the face. Then it was four o'clock; the English went to tea and we were saved." I had not quite believed him but I got the message.

A small shadow drifted across my face; a hawk was riding the wind close above us, hovering with an occasional, fluttering wing beat, the fierce head questing. I mused and recalled my early impression of Turkish pashas, lying on couches and surrounded by lush concubines and slavish attendants. Now that we had toured Constantinople, I had glimpsed the reality, seen the hard-bitten people, strong peasants from the mountains of Anatolia and swarthy fishermen, and vast numbers of mobile vegetable stalls in endless markets.

We had visited some mosques and a memory jerked me out of my daze, as the hawk swooped on some cowering prey on the hillside below us. Tom and Simon stood in a reverential silence, which I broke.

"The last mosque we saw, was it the one of Suleiman the Magnificent? Sort of changed my view. I'd always looked on Islam as a noisy, hostile horde beating at the gates of Europe, but there was a very peaceful atmosphere there."

"Yes," said Simon, "it comes from the silence, thick carpets, no shoes, a soundproofed door..."

Tom broke in, "And the absence of representational art, the separation of men from women. You can't concentrate on holy things with a stained-glass window picturing some saint slaying a dragon, above you and a pretty girl's bum above the kneeler in front of you."

Simon picked it up. "The Great Mogul, Emperor of India, Baber, got it right. 'Sometimes I go to the Mosque, sometimes to the Hindu Temple, sometimes to the Christian Church.' A pity more people don't have those ideas and, actually, one English translation of Islam is Peace."

Then he changed tack. "It's a bit strange that we three are the only ones walking this battlefield; all the others are lolling on the beach. What an amateurish crowd. I wish we had time to walk to the end of the ridge and view Suvla Bay – that is where we nearly made it." He paused in recollection. "Our attackers, mostly Anzacs, had got to the crest of the ridge to cut off the whole peninsula. Three things stopped them, a barrage of fifteen inch shells from a supporting battleship fell on **our** own front line troops, our reserves had been sent off to bathe in the sea and the opposing scratch battalion of gendarmerie were commanded by a brigadier, who happened to be the best soldier in Europe." He paused dramatically, "Mustafa Kemal."

This gave me food for thought. Simon may have exaggerated about Mustafa Kemal but what else had the latter done? – ejected the Sultanate and the victorious allies and forged the rump of the Ottoman Empire into an impregnable, secular state, lying on the frontiers of Europe, Asia and Africa.

I looked down on the Dardanelles out through which were flowing the waters of the Danube and the great rivers of the Central Russian upland. The shadow of a cloud passed over us and there was a chill in the wind. Simon looked up at the sun and remarked, "We had better turn back. The ship's boats will be in to pick us up at three o'clock."

Just after we turned, my foot caught a hard object hidden in among the tussocks. An unexploded shell rolled into view. Tom bent to examine it.

"It was fired from a British destroyer, lucky it didn't go off, explosives get unstable in their old age, like human beings."

I had a sudden mood swing, sensing the presence of those thousands of young men, who had died here so uselessly; a microcosm of the millions who had died on the Western Front, their eagerness for the future stilled so prematurely, with frightful suffering for many. Somehow we should see that this could never happen again. I had fallen into a dream-like trance, in which I must have put some of my thoughts into words, for it seemed to be apropos of nothing that Tom said:

"Wars are caused principally by pacifism, parsimony and pusillanimous politicians."

Tom was in a passing phase of cultivating alliteration. He continued:

"Si vis pacem, para bellum. If you wish for peace, prepare for war."

I had long ago memorised that Latin tag without seeing the point, which, now became crystal clear after many earbashings from Tom. We walked back towards the beach, past some clumps of grass pushing up through the ribcage of a long-dead horse or pack-mule. As we slithered down to the beach, the picnickers waved derisively. One chap who knew Tom's idiosyncrasies, shouted, "Keen, clean and conscientious."

Simon muttered, "Silly cunts," which surprised me for he normally never used coarse language.

The ship's boats took us off the beach to the destroyer, her anchor already at short stay and we were quickly under way. Eight bells (4 p.m.) struck and the boatswain's mate called, "Hands to tea," just like in 1915!

We slipped round into the straits for a two hundred mile trip through the Dardanelles, the Sea of Marmora and the entry to our anchorage in the Bosporus. I was tired but had no wish to sleep. I asked permission from the Officer of the Watch and propped myself up on the wing of the destroyer's open bridge, watching the winking lights of the fishing boats and the outlines of the hills against the stars.

About halfway across the Marmora a small power-driven boat, with no fishing lights, came in on our port (left-hand) side on a steady bearing. I could see her green starboard (right-hand) light. By the international rules for avoiding collisions at sea, she was bound to give way, to alter course and pass under our stern in plenty of time. She just kept coming on.

Our captain had been called to the bridge and ordered some terse sound signals with the steam siren. The boat came on, unswervingly. At the last moment, our captain gave a curse and, with full helm putting the inner propeller astern and making the appropriate sound signal, shaved under the stern of the miscreant, now clearly illuminated by our Aldis signalling lamp. I could see a huge, hawk-faced man at the helm, making an obscene gesture.

We came to our anchorage at dawn. The Hunter of the East had caught the Sultan's turret in a noose of light.

Chapter Seven

Hong Kong – Early 1930s

Life sprang into top gear when I secured an appointment as First Lieutenant, Second-in-Command – ("Jimmy" in naval argot) – to a submarine on the China Station. Effort was needed to get this appointment. I had pulled myself painfully together halfway through my time as a junior officer in submarines and had earned a goodish report and also had paid circumspect visits to the appropriate officer to get myself earmarked for the China station. Tom was the Third Officer in a sister submarine. Our flotilla, now consisting of nine boats, was the sole defence in the Far East against the rising expansionist power of Japan's main fleet. Simon was a signals officer on the staff of the Commander-in-Chief.

We reunited with immense joy on board "Medway", the great submarine depot ship, built specially for the job, giving unaccustomed comfort and repair facilities to the submarines. Simon had shot up in height and was now good-looking by any standard. Tom, of medium height and finely drawn, had intelligent humour in his eyes and grace in his movement. I was shortish, stocky, too beefy for a gymnast, ruddy faced, eager.

Over a few quick gins in the mess we decided to make a night of it – a run ashore. Tom was now able to afford a splurge, an old cousin who owned a pub had taken over the finances of his mother. We, the submariners, earned the princely sum of six shillings a day as submarine pay. Simon was now the poor man but we were standing duty-free drinks on board our own ship. Simon was dressed for shore, so Tom and I bounded off to our cabins and climbed into our shore-going, drinking suits. Everything was speeding up in a flurry of friendship. As we ran down the ladder to the quarterdeck, I shouted into the dark harbour for "Sampan Mary". A slim graceful boat glided up to the gangway rowed with a stern oar, the "yulow", by a remarkably handsome, middle-aged Chinese woman. Her two pretty, giggling daughters scampered around doing the crew work – an old crone sat silent at the stern, puffing an opium pipe. Somewhere stowed under the floor boards was, I knew, a baby – ('cheese eye' was the nearest I could get to the Chinese word for child). Mary was under contract to us. She ferried us ashore, had the right to collect, pick over and dispose of all our refuse and earned a monthly pittance. Her daughters polished the brass air vents on the submarine saddle tanks, using their feet on the cloths with a rotating motion, as they exchanged cheeky repartee with the sailors. Now in the dark, all was silent until we shoved off and the girls raised the wing-like, fully battened sail. "Hong Kong side," I said. Mary pushed over the tiller and we sprang into the night towards the Island, the dark hills girt with necklaces of lights.

During the short journey, our lives were suddenly put somewhat at risk. One of the many "Walla Wallas", (small motor boats which threatened to make obsolete the picturesque sampans), charged out of the night showing no lights and with a fine disdain for the rule of the road at sea, neglected to give way to us and came in on a collision course. At the last instant, Mary let out a curse and made a violent alteration of course to avoid destruction. To add to the risk and fear, she had to pass close under the villain's stern, thus cutting off any devils which might be following him and transferring them to us; a considerable loss of face was involved. I had risen in alarm and stood beside the old lady, who removed her pipe and grunted in my ear, "Bouhao" – (not good) – an understatement I thought and supplemented "Ting bouhao" – (very not good).

"The triumph," said Simon, "of the mechanical age over sail." I caught a glimpse of two figures in European dress, sitting in the stern sheets of the Walla Walla. More than impervious to all this danger and bad manners, they turned their faces away. One, I noticed, had a square head, with hair *en brosse*. It was too trivial to wonder deeply if they were ashamed of their driver or wished not to be recognised. I shivered to think of what would have befallen the *cheese-eye*, if we had crashed.

Suddenly we came into the glare of lights around the landing jetty. Mary, instead of lowering the sail, simply slackened it away to weathercock itself, the battened panels fluttering without fuss as no white man's sail could. Judging to within a few inches, she curved silently alongside, the girls had to make no effort with their bamboo boat hooks as we stepped ashore. Tom had already learnt a little Cantonese and was able to exchange friendly chat with Mary.

In the bar of the Hong Kong Club, we formed a quiet trio, distancing ourselves from older members, some of whom appeared to be ossified. "The last of the dinosaurs," whispered Tom. I was still seething with indignation about our near miss in the harbour. "That swine nearly cut us down and what was he doing without lights, trying to hide?"

"No," said Simon, "just bad manners and arrogance – but only a bad man would behave like that – probably he is in with smugglers or piracy; the pirates are only just round the corner in Bias Bay. I don't suppose he'd go outside the harbour in that boat but he might be contacting pirate junks up near Lye Mun Pass; and those two chaps in the stern sheets, God knows they could be anyone or any race; but the big chap looked European."

We chatted on, mostly filling in the gaps left by our separated lives, since our earlier days in the Mediterranean fleet, and planning a glorious binge of Chinese food in the South China Hotel. "Last drinks," said Simon, "I can't wait for food – walk there, rickshaw home."

The South China Hotel was in festive array. A Chinese warlord had slipped over the border, knowing he would have to be out in twenty-four hours, being *persona non grata* in the colony. He had taken a whole floor to make the most of his time in feasting and drinking. The Chinese are, contrary to their image of inscrutability, a nation with outgoing vitality and humour; their style of cooking and serving endless little dishes of surpassing flavour and balance lends itself to banquets. The noise from this orgy was extremely clamorous, so we sought a quiet refuge away from it and well screened off. A succession of eye-catching, exotic foods arrived and endless tiny cups of unsweetened green tea.

We had gossiped a great deal and I wanted to stimulate the others to talk. My role had always been that of Dr Watson.

"What, Tom," I said, "do you think is the cause and meaning of all this stir-up in Germany, strange fusses in Italy and Japan, already at war in Manchuria and Jehol, strange new creeds and talk of socialism all over the place?"

Tom laid down his chopsticks and thought a while: "Socialism is social engineering, social surgery, meant to cure some ailment. Communism is, we are told in Russia, socialism achieved, a substitute religion; national socialism is sweeping Germany. All these forces can only be controlled by discipline. What is the nature of Fascism? The fasces was the symbol of the Roman legion, discipline, a bundle of rods with an axe in the middle. A bundle, bound tight, is stronger than the individual rod. I don't know if the axe was for cutting the rods or for cutting up you – the dissenter. When people lose their sense of social security, they tend to revert to tribalism, the absolute tribal chief with a witch doctor at his elbow – the rule of war is brought into government – the end justifies the means."

"So," said Simon, "you think that all these amount to the same thing and the tribes, are they on the warpath?"

Tom took a few ruminative bites of chicken and bean shoots. "What was the principal cause of the 1914 war? The invention of the dreadnought, with rotating gun turrets, made all previous ships obsolete, so the great British superiority in ship numbers was overtaken at one bound. The British then cut their battleship building programme, hoping Germany would do the same. The Germans saw the chance to outbuild us in *modern* ships. The completion of the Kiel Canal to carry big ships opened the Baltic for quick, strategic movements to the North Sea."

"So, it's just a repetition of history," broke in Simon. "The merchant nations which wished for peace, let their guards down, like, for instance, the cities of the plain of the Tigris and Euphrates – which got zapped twice by the Mongols. But *now* where does this lead us? The Washington Treaty limited the building of battleships to 35,000 tons and a ratio of 5:5:3 between USA, UK and Japan. Germany was disarmed at Versailles. There has been no war for ten years. But, again, all the old ships are out-of-date and Japan humiliated."

"And," said Tom, "a battleship to carry a main armament, a huge anti-aircraft armament, a proper armoured citadel, and to have a high speed must be at least 60,000 tons. A battleship is not an obsolete conception; it just hasn't been kept up-to-date." This all sounded somewhat disconnected to me and I'd heard some of it before. I could not measure up battleships to Genghis Khan and my eye became deflected by a pretty Chinese waitress with a slit skirt. Suddenly, remembering the incident of the flagship carpeted with bumph, I exclaimed, "But what about aircraft carriers?"

"Yes," said Tom, "lots and lots of carriers, but do you know why Charles I had his head cut off?"

I was just about to mention something about the Divine Right of Kings, when he continued:

"Because the English people did not want to pay 'ship money', a blanket poll tax."

Talk then turned to our plans to sail to Macau, the Portuguese colony to the south, to cruise to Mirs Bay, opposite the pirates' lair, to climb Sha-tao-Kok, the steep mountain on the border, and how we would mount an expedition into mainland China. Here we were, on the rim of the Eastern world, the sunset beckoned into Asia.

We were immensely satisfied by the meal, the crisp vegetables retaining their full flavour, fish which had been kept alive in flooded compartments in junks – fresh-killed, sea-tasting; duck which had swum down the Pearl River a hundred miles, cooked so that nothing was lost from it; by comparison our naval food had tasted like flannel. We rose, gratefully, paid our bills with merry farewells and walked out to the waiting rickshaws.

Tom was returning to the ship, Simon to his shore quarters, high on the Peak above the town. We said goodnight and I after a moment's hesitation, said to the rickshaw coolie "Happy Valley". A grin broke over his face and he trotted off, hawked and spat and said "I savvy, Missie Ethel Mergen's", a tolerated house, where I knew there was a recent arrival, young, pretty, called "The Canada Chick".

We drew up to a nondescript building and I tapped on the door. A light went on over my head and a trap door opened behind which was a grille from where I was scrutinised. The door opened and I went in to a scene of merriment. Ethel, Germanic, strong, middle-aged, still good-looking, gave me a loud welcome. A party was in progress.

Chapter Eight
Hong Kong – Early 1930s (continued)

I was at the bottom of a deep, dark well, swimming up for the surface, lungs bursting. An admonitory, magisterial finger wagged at my face and a rescuing hand clutched my shoulder. The hand shook me insistently. I awoke, and leaning over me was an elderly, ugly, hunchbacked Chinese man. I recognised Wong, Ethel's major-domo, shroff, debt collector. He thrust a mug of steaming tea, from which arose a scent of good Scotch whisky, into my shaking hand. I sipped gratefully, assuaging the appalling taste and feeling in my mouth. Then realising that I was in a double bed turned to look at my companion who was not, as I had supposed, the "Chick" but Ethel; great heavens, old enough to be my mother! She had woken and, sitting up with naked bosom and unashamed in front of Wong, seized from him the proffered second cup of tea, similarly laced, and said, "What time Wong?"

Wong who *did* live up to the image of Chinese inscrutability, replied, "Seven o'clock, missie," passed her a bed jacket and withdrew without noise.

"Well, sailor," said Ethel between sips, "we had to fool you; you had had a lot of whisky and a very important visitor wanted 'the Chick'. I could not refuse."

"Well, who was he?" I said crossly, guessing that someone had put a Mickey in my drink.

"Oh, a Dutch baron. Van Winblen or something, just down from Mongolia, where he buys China ponies from the Khans, sells them for polo ponies and also, believe it or not, to the US army. They must be fighting the Indians again."

I shrugged off the previous night, being unable to make anything of it. Had I really slept, even mated with the old girl? Tea and whisky were clearing my head.

"God I have to get going quick, I must be on board by eight." I flung on my clothes which beautifully folded by Wong, lay on a chair. Ethel looked at me quizzically, and drawled "not ba-a-d."

Guessing that there were sleepers, I tiptoed out onto the dark landing in my socks to find the bathroom and then froze. There was a noise on the stairway. a man had come out of one of the rooms and was making for the front door; I saw him clearly as the daylight caught him. Tall, well-made, with handsome features set in a ruthless expression; a white scar across his cheekbone showed vividly against his deeply-tanned face. His blond, short-cut hair showed the shape of the back of his head, which reminded me of something I could not place. Well it was no good crying; he had taken the pretty 'Chick' and I was left with a sour hangover.

I completed dressing and slicked my hair with Ethel's comb. Wong produced a rickshaw and I made a quick decision about my next move. My submarine was refitting in the dockyard. I had no uniform on board her and I could not retreat down there. I knew that some of the top brass liked to parade the "Medway's" deck to check on young officers, who came offshore at that time and had obviously been up to no good. "Cricket Club," I shouted to my pilot. I had left a singlet and running shorts in my locker at the Cricket Club a day or so previously. After changing into these, my short run to the jetty, on top of a very lowlife evening, rendered me puce and sweating as though I had run to the top of the Peak ramps some fifteen hundred feet up; a condition which was sustained until the sampan drew alongside the depot ship. I sprinted smartly up the gangway, giving the impression of a man dedicated to early morning fitness.

Later that day, when I retrieved my suit from the Club, I found an ill-written note in the pocket, "Come Wednesday afternoon three. Chick." It was Saturday. I counted the hours from then till Wednesday 3 p.m.

As my boat was undergoing her long refit in dry dock there was no difficulty in getting away on Wednesday afternoon. Presenting myself at Ethel's door, I was let in and surprised to find the Chick alone; the house was otherwise empty. She looked ravishing to me and indeed she was still young enough not to have been raddled by her frightful life; perhaps she was one of those fortunate people who have a constitution which can put up with a lot of abuse. All she said was "Hallo, Bob" and giggled. I don't think she knew anything else. She led me upstairs to her room. I went to take her in my arms but stopped as I heard a car draw up at the front door. A look of terror spread over the girl's face. "Quick," she said, and knelt down, pulling away a corner of a drugget carpet and lifting a concealed trap door in the floorboards. Beneath us there was a shallow compartment between the floor of our room and the ceiling below. Into this, spurred by her frantic whispers, I crawled, following her as a key rattled in the front door. Our lid was noiselessly lowered. The drugget carpet must have dropped into place. We lay side-by-side in what was, an old brothel trick, an eyrie for voyeurs to look down and enjoy, vicariously, the pleasures of others. I was alarmed by Chick's obvious fear and concentrated on keeping still and quiet. There was no peephole within my view. There was a noise of tramping round the house and then I realised that the room beneath us was being occupied.

I could hear every word of the subsequent conversation between two men below us. It was so shattering to me that I felt that the beating of my heart would betray us.

Both voices spoke in very good, though stilted, educated English, evidently their common tongue, one spoke with a slightly guttural accent – I will call him Colonel C. The other had a minute amount of sibilance in his speech, slightly cracked, probably by age. He will be Admiral A. I remember the conversation accurately, as I put it down on paper later that day, and this is how it went.

C. "Lord Admiral, welcome to Hong Kong, will you honour me by taking a glass of this excellent Scotch whisky, which the thoughtful Wong has provided."

A. "Colonel Baron, it is I who am honoured by your invitation and hospitality. May I, however, enquire why we meet in this place which appears to me to be what you would call a house of ill fame?"

There was a noise of liquid splashing into glasses and of the two men rising and clicking their heels.

C. "I drink to the Rising Sun".

A. "To greater Germany".

There was earnest fervour in their voices; they resumed their seats and dialogue.

C. "This house is completely safe and I have arranged for it to be empty all this afternoon. The people here are the only ones in the colony in my complete confidence."

A. "Although our positions entitle us, indeed enjoin us, to maximise our pleasure with the polite conversation of gentlemen, the importance of our mission and the short time at our disposal compels us to come at once to grips with our problems."

C. "Perhaps, as the junior and younger man I should be permitted to speak first, do you agree, Admiral?"

A. "Proceed then please."

C. "Our situation is tantalising and yet has so much possibility but so many frustrations. Our country is, at last, rising to greatness under its new leader; we are all determined that this will be so. Our progression to overwhelming strength is assured. Of the other powers, America is asleep, France rotted by socialism, Russia rent by the fears of their ruler and the ruler's fears of his own people and Britain is disarmed; two divisions, a joke."

A. "But the British fleet?"

C. "Obsolete and it can't penetrate into Europe. When we move we will be confident of victory.

Now I come to the unfortunate part, our group, which is certain of the rightness of its Grand Strategy, is yet unable to carry with us those who will be able to sway the staff and the leaders. This is our plan. France and the rest of Europe will be rubbed out, Britain neutralised. Russia is too big and cold to be grabbed. We do not want to confront the whole of Russia. When we move east, we want a single, fast, overwhelming thrust to the south of the Pripet Marshes, through the Ukraine, where the people long to throw off their yoke and will join with us, through the Caucusus, where they still smart from the Russian Conquest and through Persia, the Gulf, the oilfields to Aden. So far, other counsels have prevailed."

A. "Herr Baron, I was not deceived; my informers told me that you and I were like hand to glove. The only thing which matters in war is the right Grand Strategy; all else is detail.

You and I are in exactly the same position and our ideas coincide except for the small detail that we need Aden for our fleet. We do not want to awaken the American sleeping giant nor confront him. Our way is down the China coast, the flank protected by shore-based aircraft, and then to take out Singapore, Ceylon and join you in the Gulf."

If the British are threatened at home they will never send the main fleet to Singapore.

We are, however, I suspect, in exactly the same position as you. People in control are deceiving the Emperor. Confrontation on a large scale is in their minds. Is my interpretation of your dilemma correct? – that there is a plan to try to swallow up these icy, northern wastes."

C. "I will not detail the plan, but it is even worse than you describe."

A. "Rather than throw our country into disaster, I would favour a peace party, which has also the Emperor's favour. Have you any such option?"

C. "Well a short answer is best – no."

A. "As well as working behind the scenes for the adoption of our plan we have an agent in the field: one of the very highest quality who works, far above the realms of common spying, in measuring the very heartbeats of nations and on influencing the minds of men who may sway the moods of whole peoples."

C. "He must be, then, of extraordinary quality. We have many agents, but none as you describe, and will he, your agent, be totally dedicated to the evolution of your plan?"

A. "Yes, and when we have a ring of steel across the Indian Ocean and round the Eurasian land mass, the interior will fall to pieces like a ripe fruit. The Russian and Chinese empires will split into their original ethnic segments, likewise the Indian subcontinent. Satraps can be put in and Africa retribalised, a line drawn between us."

C. "Where is the line?"

A. "Colonel we are discussing, surely, Grand Strategy. In any case our plans can go no further until we can get the acceptance of our leaders. To that we must surely work with all our force and subtlety. This short meeting has encouraged me towards this end. I regret that my age prevents me from meeting you on your own rugged ground on the mainland. This hole-in-the-corner business is repugnant to me, but necessary."

C. "To me, also, and the fact that it is undesirable for us to meet in our own countries or in public, where we are watched and suspected to a certain extent: both our movements are being driven underground."

A. "So now we must depart and slip away across the border, we don't even have to know our separate routes. I trust your assurance that this house is not watched."

Both men then made formal farewells and left the house. The car moved away. As we scrambled out of our retreat, I caught sight of a plugged knothole in the floor. I was not able to resist removing the plug and looking down; below was a double bed. I noticed, as we emerged, that there was no dust on us. Chick was shaking and tearful.

"God," she said, "I could have my throat cut. I was told to make myself scarce this afternoon on pain of – ugh! My memory has gone to fluff. I thought it was to be some private sex orgy. What was all that baloney the two old geezers were spouting?" She sobbed on, "Now we have to get out quick. We should be OK. They have some way of seeing the house is not spied on – just go Bob – move."

I returned to the depot ship, frustrated, puzzled and not a little alarmed. I sat later in my cabin writing my notes on the conversation in the bordel and thought of my options. One was to thrash the thing out with my more intelligent friends, and the second was to report it to my captain, Fred Mailing, for transmission, through the proper channels, to higher authority.

My first option was closed to me. I found that Tom's submarine had been sent at short notice to Cheefoo, a port in north China, where a local warlord was threatening to advance on and sack the town. Simon was seconded to go with them to represent the staff and provide extra communication. Fifty years after the event it seems incredible that this vast country should have been in such chaos that gunboat diplomacy could have been possible, needful and probably effective. So they were away.

Fred Malling was a good average submarine commander at sea. In harbour and, particularly, during the refit, he drank heavily. I had forgotten that he had a puritan streak in his outlook.

I tapped on the door of my CO's cabin in the depot ship and entered.

"Ah, Number One," he said, "get yourself a glass from the cupboard and take a chair. What do you want to see me about?"

I sat down, looked into his face, magnificent but drink-smitten, and, without preamble, told him the whole story as I have written it down here. During this, the tide in the whisky bottle ebbed fast. Malling leant forward, he had dropped his book:

"First of all, Number One, let me tell you that your conduct in visiting such a house as you describe is not becoming an officer and a gentleman. To be birtling with whores is nothing short of disgusting." His face curved in a rictus of displeasure. "Apart from immorality and setting a bad example, you run the risk of catching VD and public disgrace, not to mention the well-deserved agony of treatment. I can't control your private life, but I can seriously consider whether you should serve under my command." I moved uneasily at that, though I did not think that he would carry out his threat. "You were correct to bring it to my notice, but these strange characters, on whom you were able to eavesdrop, are obviously cowboy adventurers. They are self-confessed *persona non grata* with their governments. In any case, talk of assaulting Singapore is ridiculous. The place is to be made impregnable with casemated fifteen inch guns. As to talk of strangling the whole of Asia, they must be demented. Now I am certainly not going to bother the intelligence staff with such poppycock. They have all they can do to keep tabs on Chinese pirates."

"But, Sir," I said lamely, "should not Ethel Mergen's place be watched?"

"I am quite sure the police have that well in hand and I wish you to forget the whole beastly business. Now Number One, I am pleased with your work and I want you from now on to keep out of mischief and simply banish all that farrago from your mind."

I rose a bit stiffly and said "aye, aye, sir" and withdrew. I intended that these orders would not be fully obeyed. There were other houses of tolerance which could be explored.

I suppose the reason that, in my unpardonable stupidity, I took the matter no further was compounded by several factors: the departure of my friends, the tradition of unquestioning loyalty to the captain, possibly the threat of removal from the ship and probably from the submarine service but certainly the fact that, immediately after this, I was struck by a new, devastating bombshell, which blew other matters from my mind.

Chapter Nine

The Tiger Hunt

The dockyard siren wailed for closing time. The sound of hammers chipping the paint and rust in the saddle tanks died away. The submarine was silent, damp and smelly from the rotting shellfish which had been scraped off her hull and lay in the bottom of the dry dock. I remembered that I had promised to have a drink with Bumble Harp, whose submarine was lying alongside the wall inside the dockyard basin. As I walked across the dockyard, I also remembered that I intended to borrow, from Bumble, one of his rifles for a forthcoming shooting competition, our rifles having been returned to the armament depot for the duration of the refit. I had been shipmates in a previous commission with Lofty Morgan, gun layer of the submarine which I was asked to visit and I knew that he would pick me a good rifle and tell me exactly how it performed.

Lofty was the naval nickname for a tall man; Morgan, christened Loftus, was diminutive. He met me on the gangway with his inevitable grin, discussed the merits of the rifle and promised to tighten up "the furniture", meaning the woodwork of the weapon. Then he said, "Bit of a party going on below, sir. There's a skirt; a real corker." I slid down the fore-hatch ladder with this information ringing in my ears and turned to walk down the narrow corridor into the officers' quarters. I pulled aside the curtain, which gave a little privacy to the wardroom, from whence issued a hum of conversation.

As time goes on one is bound to see a vast number of beautiful women, read descriptions of feminine loveliness, hackneyed or poetic; but nothing in my experience had prepared me for the bolt of lightning which struck me as I came face to face with Lee O'Connor across the wardroom table. She had been playing tennis with an officer on the staff, who lounged magnificently at the end of the room. I forget his name, one of those chaps who never puts a foot wrong; I foretold that he would become an admiral in due course. I knew that he played tennis at a very high standard and that for a girl to play singles with him meant that she must have a top class skill. The loveliness of the girl lay mostly in her health and bone structure, probably inherited from bloodlines of country people; her physique combined the grace of Diana, the huntress, with Aphrodite, the goddess of love; I noticed the epicanthic fold of her upper eyelid; she must have been partly Chinese.

There were a couple of other men sitting round the table, both civilians and much older than the rest of us; one looked like a Taipan businessman, the other professorial, probably from Hong Kong University. I felt overawed and thought I would become tongue-tied, but not at all. Lee engaged me in conversation at once and we discovered a mutual interest in adventurous sport. I had found an outlet in sailing the naval depot officer's yacht "Tavy II" round the Island of Hong Kong. Lee had done some ocean racing and recounted gaily how the yacht, in which she crewed, had approached a crowd of junks anchored in a bay in one of the off-shore islands. The junks, fearing the silent approach of the ubiquitous pirates, had fired a canon containing grapeshot. Fortunately, it was sighted too high and the spinnaker, riddled with holes, its halliard severed, collapsed and fluttered down on the deck. Only Lee's fluent command of Cantonese and frantic shouts saved the yacht from further attack.

We chatted, happy and relaxed. The Chinese steward and his unofficial helper "Makee Learn" answered the calls for rounds of drinks. They were northerners, from Shantung, speaking a broader dialect than the local Cantonese. Lee made a remark in their own language, which had them both in fits of laughter, but I noticed that she nursed her glass and was not served with more drink. The Taipan, looking slightly disapproving at this badinage, remarked apropos of nothing, "I saw in the paper this morning that a tiger has been seen in the new territories."

"Yes," said the professor, "they very occasionally wander out here. I fear that it's a rogue and may do damage to stock, perhaps to humans but I doubt that; there has not been any official response. It seems to be in the area of Ma On Shan."

"Let's shoot it," I said, not expecting anyone to respond. There was a general demurring; no one had time for such nonsense, except

Lee, who looked straight at me and said, "All right, Bob, I'll go with you."

"Well, you can't go now," said Bumble. "It's getting dark."

There was a pause and Lee said, "There is a full moon and clear sky. There is a path over the Kowloon hills with paving stones, which show up in the moonlight, and surely Bob has a torch."

The staff officer protested, "Well, you can't walk ashore with a rifle; the police on the jetty would jump you."

I recalled my capacious golf bag in which a rifle could easily be camouflaged and so the crazy scheme was hatched. Lee would go across to the mainland in the ferry and to her flat in Kowloon to get ready. I would go off to the depot ship, moored to a buoy in the middle of the harbour, carrying the rifle, change my clothes, get the golf bag and then go over to Kowloon and meet her.

There was fresh discussion about ammunition. Large animals are shot with soft-nosed bullets. The Lee Enfield ·303, which saw us through the 1914 war and was to do the same in the later struggle, fired a hard-nosed shot. Bumble suggested cutting nicks in the noses of a few bullets to cause them to expand.

"No," I said, "I don't trust that sort of missile to fly straight."

Bumble reminded me that although I was an excellent shot I was nowhere nearly as good as the chief engine room artificer in our team; he put every shot through the bull's-eye.

"Agreed," I replied, "but that is from lying on a mat with the rifle supported. When I was a kid I could hit a moving rabbit with a ·22."

Someone remarked, crossly, "Well you must be crazy, it's a thousand to one you will see a tiger."

With that the guests dispersed.

I stayed a while with Bumble. "Of course you are smitten by Lee," he said "everyone is, but there is nothing doing; she is incredibly bright; has strings of letters after her name from universities in England, USA, Hong Kong and all over. She is related to the aristocracy and moves everywhere in high circles. No one gets her to wed or bed and, Bob, don't be deceived by the fact that she looks a lot younger than you – actually she is quite a bit older."

"Well," I said, "it does not seem fair that someone should have everything handed to them on a plate, and why didn't I meet her before?"

Bumble grinned, "You just move in a different environment, your boat, booze-ups, Ethel's and sailing."

As I rose to leave, Lofty, who had overheard all the conversation and had been busy "tightening up the furniture", appeared from behind the curtain carrying the rifle and a pocket of ammo, unnicked. "At two hundred yards she will hit the top right-hand corner of the bull," he explained, earnestly. "Aim at the droop of his left whisker."

I walked along the dockyard basin wall and called softly into the night. Presently there was a splash and the sampan nosed up to the wall. I pointed towards the depot ship and a faint breeze carried us across the silent water.

No one thought it strange that I carried a rifle over the gangway, nor later, when I descended with a golf bag over my shoulder; it might have been assumed that I was depositing it ashore for a game next day. The rifle nestled coyly among the clubs.

As we made for Kowloon on the Chinese mainland, Mary was unusually silent and preoccupied. She aided the sail by strokes of her stern oar, the "yulow". Suddenly she spat over the side and ejaculated, "Typhoon come."

"Nonsense Mary," I said, "no typhoon warning signal, no wind or rain."

She burst into a torrent of mixed pidgin and Cantonese. The girls up forward were unusually quiet. The old woman impassive in the stern, puffed at her pipe. I caught the words "Typhoon flies". I noticed some of those ungainly insects fluttering over the water as I jumped ashore at Kowloon. Mary quickly pushed off from the jetty and made towards the typhoon shelter for small craft.

I shouldered the heavy golf bag and walked behind the imposing, newly-built Peninsula Hotel and rang the doorbell of the flat to which I had been directed. Lee opened the door and led me upstairs into an L-shaped room. The long arm of the L was an austerely furnished living room; the short arm a library, floor to ceiling with bookshelves, housing ranks of books in a wide variety of languages. Perched on the arm of a large easy chair in the living room was a small wizened Chinese woman who looked old enough to be the mother of the crone who sat in the stern sheets of Mary's sampan. She appeared to be scolding Lee, with a machine gun fire of verbiage, in a language which did not seem to resemble Cantonese. When she paused for breath, I tried to address her in English but she had none of it. I imagined the old girl was talking some dialect from out in the sticks, perhaps Mongolia.

I said to Lee, "What language is this?"

"Irish," she replied, "Amah has almost forgotten her mother tongue. She lived for twenty years in the Gaelic-speaking district of West Connaught."

Lee was ready, dressed in a bush shirt and slacks; we both had torches. I got the gun out and left the golf bag with the old scold, slung the rifle on my shoulder and pocketed the ammo. We set off into the night which was unnaturally still and warm. We moved easily through the crowds in the back streets of Kowloon. No one looked askance at my firearm and the population thinned out as we went. The track across the Kowloon Hills to the right of Lion rock was easy; the paving stones set at frequent intervals shone like jewels in the bright moonlight. Then there was a long haul over Buffalo Hill and another amorphous lump beyond where the going was rougher, we had to use our torches and peer at the outline of the hills against the stars. The pace became slow and we kept our breath for walking. The soil up in those hills is very poor and there were no farms or livestock. As we drew up at last under the bulk of Ma-on-Shan, the hunchback mountain which slopes down to Tolo Harbour, a Chinese fjord, the atmosphere became hazy and there was a soughing, fluctuating breeze. Lee produced a small pocket compass.

I was beginning to tire and remarked, "We must be crazy to hope to find an animal in the New Territories, which cover about a hundred square miles of land."

Lee replied, "There are one or two feral goats, which graze the top of Ma-on-Shan. If the tiger was reported in that area all the farm stock will be shut in. Those goats will be a bait. Let's make for the top, there is a good path."

"The torches will frighten the animal away or, worse, perhaps draw him to us in the darkness."

"Well," she said, "you will have to take a pot shot."

I stopped and put a clip of shells in the magazine and one up the spout. As we struggled up the steep winding path the dawn came up behind us, yellow and hideous. We reached the rounded cap of the mountain, slightly separated. Lee was a little ahead and below me. Some hundred feet above and to my right I saw a black goat grazing.

It lifted its head and froze, looking down the hillside; then I saw the tiger, below and coming up straight towards us.

He was slightly lame on his right foreleg and looked mangy, unlike tigers I had seen in zoos and circuses and pictures. He was growling horribly and shaking his head from side to side. Lee stood quite still. When the beast got within about fifty paces, I fired and hit it in the leg which was already lame. The bullet must have drilled a neat hole and slowed it not at all, but infuriated it further.

I saw that Lee would mask my fire and I shouted to her to drop. As she crouched, the tiger charged at her and reared up for its final pounce, about twenty paces from me. I shot into the brain through its open mouth. It looked enormous, as it clawed the air and teetered in death in a vertical position. A sudden gust of wind swept over the ridge and the dead animal fell backwards and rolled down the steep incline.

I started to shake. Lee rose, turned to me and said "Shabash, Bob", which I recognised as Hindi for "Thank you". I then realised that she was unafraid, unshocked, unmoved. I must have been as white as a sheet; her healthy flush might have proceeded from a nice game of hockey.

Then she said, "I suppose you realise that we have a typhoon on our hands; there is a farmhouse tucked into the hillside about fifteen hundred feet below us let's go."

The farmhouse was more than fifteen hundred feet further down and we had a hard time descending over the rough ground in the rapidly rising wind. The rifle became more of an encumbrance among the tussocks and in steep descent. Wracked clouds scudded overhead and there was a blackness to the southward from where the wind was coming.

The farmer was putting a bar across the door of his shed and, for good measure, rolling two large stones against it. He immediately responded to Lee and they spoke urgently in Cantonese. I recognised the words "diaphoong bou how" – big wind – not good. He beckoned us inside his house, whose back wall pressed against a terrace in the hillside and the building's outline was streamlined to the wind. The door was bolted on the inside with a great, wooden bar through wooden hasps. He turned to his family. The couple were middle-aged, their faces bronzed and seamed, wearing faded blue "coolie" trouser suits. Two small children, a boy and a girl, sat on stools and regarded us without apparent dismay at our invasion, or the threatening elemental fury without. Lee spoke reassuringly to the woman who was nervous, making some indirect remark towards the children, obviously disparaging, to avoid alerting any jealous spirits which lurk in the lower atmosphere, the latter now being very much on the move. The woman lit oil lamps, it was becoming gloomy, and she motioned us to two rattan chairs.

"What better place to sit it out? And we can award the tiger's skin to our hosts," I remarked with forced jollity. I had far from recovered from the shock of that frightful encounter on the mountain top.

The wind rose with appalling acceleration and rain battered the roof with the noise of machine gun bullets. The typhoon must have been small in area but extreme in intensity. The wind speed would cause major disruption and the rain would make floods and landslides of mud. Here we were warm and dry and the mountain was firm; there was going to be a long wait. I dozed off in my chair, tired from the long walk and sleepless night. I must have been the only person in the colony asleep at that time. I woke up, probably two or three hours later, roused by stillness.

Lee was awake and chatting to the couple. Turning to me she said, "The eye of the storm, let's go and have a look."

The door bolt was pulled back and we emerged into a world which had gone mad. The wind, clouds and rain had vanished, the sky was clear and a number of wailing birds circled overhead, a few flapping around injured on the ground, which, even at this distance, was strewn with light refuse and wreckage blown from the town.

"Look," said Lee, "the eyewall." There was a cliff of boiling, black, vapoury cloud towering thousands of feet upwards and receding from us; a yellow haze cast an unearthly light and air must have been slowly falling for small pieces of paper and leaves pattered down round us.

The farmer gave a cry of dismay. His gardens were ruined; plants blown out of the ground or buried in mud and wind wrack. It seemed incredible that we were in a calm with a maelstrom hurtling around us and bringing frightful destruction. I looked in the direction of Kowloon, which would now be a stricken city, to see the other side of the circular eyewall approaching out of the haze; the eye must have been about fifteen miles in diameter and moving at about forty-five knots into China.

The farmer muttered something which Lee translated as "I think we go inside."

Shortly after we had bolted the door, the wind came in at full force with appalling suddenness from the opposite, northerly direction. I had broken all records by sleeping through the front end of a typhoon and, wide-awake, I now listened to its fury. The noise rose from a scream to a dull booming roar, indicating over a hundred knots of wind speed. The most distinctive feature was the enormous variations of velocity in the gusts, which played up and down over a range of about sixty knots, giving frightful differences in pressure and vacuum, pushing and sucking at our stoutly-built, bolted door. The children were now terrified, so were the parents, so was I. I looked at Lee. She had a rapt expression on her face and speaking low, as though addressing some imaginary being, uttered one word, "Kamikaze". It meant nothing to me and I thought nothing of it at the time. As the typhonic fury died down slowly, Lee talked of her childhood in Ireland. Her mother, who was partly Chinese, had died bearing her, and her father, "Red" O'Connor, a colonel in the British Army, was killed in France in 1916. His body was never found and he was posted missing, presumed killed; he had two DSOs and an MC.

"I was brought up by my cousin, Rory, an eccentric living in a grand house in the far west of Ireland behind the mountains. He fostered me with an Irish peasant family in the fashion of the ancient Normans. This, I think, accounts in part for my good fortune in having such robust health. I just never get ill. Rory took pains over my education. One of his many unusual friends, mostly Irish artists and writers, was a priest, who had renounced the cloth but who was a brilliant academic teacher, a mathematician, linguist and historian. He educated me with individual tuition right up to when I could get a scholarship into university. I suppose he was paid in food, drink, accommodation and shooting and fishing. Rory also saw that I learned to ride Connemara ponies before I could walk."

"So did you evolve isolated, a little Lady Fauntleroy?"

"No, I played happily barefoot with barefoot children. I had the perfect childhood, walking the hills, sailing the coast in the rough, seaworthy workboats, hookers, gleotogs and pookawns. I've seen a great many sick people in cities, enough to bless my own inheritance."

The wind's roar died into a scream and its scream lessened. The rain started to fall more easily and more vertically. We had a few dollars between us, for which the family were profoundly grateful but they cheered up enormously when Lee explained about the dead tiger. They could haul it down with draught animals and have it skinned. The carcass would feed pigs, dogs and fowl and the whiskers sold as an aphrodisiac. The loss of the crop would be paid for a hundredfold. The genial cheer spread to the children. From looking like crumpled wet cloths their faces opened like flowers. Lee looked at the girl, "It's as though the prettiest little doll you ever saw could walk and talk."

The wind and rain eased away. The awful meteorological monster was charging off into China, its destructive force being weakened by the friction over the land. Perhaps it would recurve and re-emerge into the China Sea further north, just so long as it did not come back to us. Lee discussed our return journey. Why did Lee always take the lead?

"It's no use going down to the village for a bus or a car. Roads will be flooded and trees down, vehicles wrecked; we must trek back over the hills. The ground is free draining. We won't get bogged down if we take care over our route."

My masculine ego was assuaged as I shouldered the rifle, but after some hours walking, I could have done without it. I felt pleased that only two rounds were expended for Lofty to fudge in his expenditure record. Lee moved silently over the wet grass and I was able to think about the strange relationship into which I had fallen with the girl I would have given my eye teeth to take to bed; to marry if I had had any money but whom I realised was not within my reach as such and also that any romantic approach would spoil our friendship. Above all I did not expect her to soften, or indeed show gratitude for having saved her life. "Thank you" was all I got. I remembered the shouts of "Shabash" by soldiers of the Indian regiments, when their side scored a goal at hockey or polo. I had thought it meant good shot. Well it was a good shot, close range but the brain is a small, difficult target when moving.

The path over the Kowloon Hills was muddy but passable. Nothing had prepared me for the scene of destruction in Kowloon and Hong Kong. The trees and bushes were wind stripped, The floods had mainly drained off; the streets, which were littered with roof tiles, broken glass, wrecked motor vehicles, rickshaws, dead dogs and a few human corpses, were not yet cleared up. We got back to Lee's flat which, being on the second floor, was not flooded. Heavy typhoon shutters had preserved the rooms but not Amah's self-confidence. She had had some sort of nervous breakdown and sat staring silently at the wall. Lee wanted me to go so that she could comfort the poor old woman. I stuffed the rifle back into the bag and, as I turned away, Lee said, "We must have a game of golf or something sometime Bob. God bless and goodbye. It *was* a good shot."

I walked round the Peninsula Hotel to the waterfront, wondering how I was going to get back either across the harbour to the dockyard or to the depot ship. The ferries were clearly out of action. Even in this sheltered stretch of Kowloon a big, confused swell was still running. There were large ships up on the rocks, smaller vessels carried inland, wreckage all over the surface of the water. We had eaten a bowl of unpolished rice in the farmhouse but I was hungry. I had no money and felt I must get back to duty. Hopefully my CO would be immured in the depot ship and would not have discovered my absence. Then I saw her, behind a sheltering breakwater arm, Sampan Mary in the only calm piece of water. How had she survived in the Typhoon shelter? I felt rather than heard Mary's triumph over her correct foretelling of the tempest. There was too much rise and fall to go alongside the depot ship. Inside the dockyard basin there was a place where I could jump. The girls fended off the light craft at either end and passed up the loaded golf bag. The rifle could go straight back to Lofty for cleaning before the shooting competition and the ammo to be locked away.

The infuriating thing about the whole episode was that everyone was so shocked by the unusual disaster that no one wanted to listen to my tiger-shooting story.

Chapter Ten

Night Sail

If I had ever possessed any latent intelligence or brightness of mind it had been muffled by a life-style of sport, drink, dedication to the naval routine and sex fulfilment. Within my friendship with Simon and Tom, I was the whetstone on which they sharpened their wits; nonetheless, something therefrom must have brushed off on me and this, perhaps, matured a dormant intellect, upon which was founded my unlikely friendship with Lee O'Connor.

Of course I wanted to bed her, so would have any normal man: the amazing blend of Celtic and Asian beauty, a shining glow of perfect health and the lithe, feminine form and grace was enough to start an anchorite, let alone an over-experienced sexual libertine.

Lee had strings of academic letters after her name and a wide-ranging record of university experience across the world, of which the significance was totally closed to me. What was clear, however, from her level gaze and lack of coquetry, was the fact that there was nothing doing; that our friendship had to be based on monastic principles – St Francis and St Clare; but, God help me, for I was no saint.

Because my submarine was refitting I had plenty of spare time for a series of expeditions, which developed into a sort of *"mariage blanc"*, the French white marriage which I suppose, most people find incomprehensible but exists for one reason or another. Of course we were not married nor was there any possibility of such a thing.

Lee's time was greatly taken up by whatever she was doing at the University and certain grand functions therein and at Government House or Taipan's palaces. Our outings, therefore, had to be at her behest and, of course, like a good dog I came to the whistle.

Some time after the tiger hunt, when the typhoon devastation had been somewhat tidied, I had a note from Lee in immaculate, scholarly handwriting, "Why don't we take Tavy out for a night sail?"

Tavy II was an old wooden yawl, about forty-five feet long, a yacht belonging to the officers of HMS *Tamar*, an ex, wooden-wall warship, which was an economical housing for the shore-based staff of the Commodore Hong Kong. As a temporary member I had the option to put down on a list of those wishing to sail in her. There were few takers. A middle-aged Chinese man known as "Tavy Boy" was the ship keeper but, being prone to seasickness he could not be described as the crew.

The north-east monsoon had come in and this gave the possibility for a fast passage round Hong Kong Island. I planned to board and set off after dockyard hours, sail gently eastward up the sheltered harbour, and then, for a short stiff beat, out through the narrow Lye Mun Pass, crossing tacks in the dark with the great junks, each a separate, floating village, an island to itself. After that the wind would be free for a fast passage. Tavy Boy had the boat rigged and ready and as we made our way out of the dockyard basin and up through the crowded harbour, he was preparing a vast supper to be eaten before sailing through the pass. He was then to relapse into a seasick coma, wrapped inside a spare sail and supine in the flying spray. Why, I wondered, did he take up such a profession? Meanwhile, as the deck-mounted cook-box flared, I noticed that the low evening sunlight glinting on Lee's jet black hair was undershooting it with red. I must have stared or there was a thought transference. Without embarrassment she said calmly, "Yes, it's my red Celtic ancestry; you see the same thing in a few Aberdeen Angus cattle, black Galloway crossed with red Highland."

There was barely a sailing breeze in the harbour under the shelter of the surrounding hills. Tavy Boy dished us up a supper suitable for the occasion, sausages from a pork butcher, (I can do without the factory product), thin bacon slices smoking from charcoal and a memorable cheese omelette, crisply unlike the usual, soggy cardboard, and fried bread which shattered at a crunch. Lee and I ensconced ourselves in the cockpit, eating our picnic off crested naval plates, which must have been inherited from the days of sailing battleships.

"Tavy Boy" started the modestly powered, auxiliary engine and took the helm, motor-sailing northward up the busy harbour.

Lee looked up at the mass of Hong Kong Island rising sharply on our right to the "Peak" crest about fifteen hundred feet above us – "It was a barren place until the opium wars; two Scotsmen started it, Jardine and Matheson, now it's a vital trading centre on the rim of the Pacific. If that whole area could become cohesive, they'd really be in business."

I remembered a piece of history, "The Mainland New Territories are only leased until 1997. The water engineer told me that the colony cannot do without the water supply from the new territories and, indeed, from mainland China, so what will happen to the island?"

Lee was scrabbling up egg scraps with greasy fried bread and popped the whole thing into her mouth with her fingers. There was a fraught pause. Tavy dodged under the stern of a Foochow fishing junk. Normally a gloomy, taciturn man; his face creased with laughter at some remark which Lee made to him in Cantonese, something to do with the aroma linked with the devils following the junk.

Then she rejoined abruptly, "The British returned the northern port of Wei Hai Wei to the Chinese in 1911, but the Royal Navy is still there; the bulldog can't let go."

After a short pause she continued enigmatically "Hong Kong will change, China will change. Britain will change." Then with a switch of thought, "At one time the British Empire looked like copying the Mongols by absorbing China; a great stable Asian dominion, it might have been better, it could scarcely be worse."

I caught myself thinking how lovely she looked. I had mastered the trick of subduing my desire and banishing that train of thought, slipping passion out of my consciousness.

To anyone familiar with Hong Kong in the 1990s, with serried ranks of tower blocks housing the burgeoning millions, the city of the 1930s might have been on another planet. Barely half a million people inhabited the Island and adjacent mainland New Territories. On the island, a picturesque, little, early Victorian town adjoined Wanchai, the Chinese quarter. On the Mainland, the vast, newly-built Peninsula Hotel nestled against the serrated backdrop of the Kowloon Hills. All these then glided past us as dusk fell. The beat to windward out through the pass was a battle. We dodged among the junks, which displayed a certain disregard for the rule of the road at sea and a desire to pass close ahead of us and thereby to transfer to us their devils. In so doing they gave us a strong whiff of decayed fish, acrid cargo and sanitary disposal. The functional sheer of their workmanlike hulls and the shell-like curve of their handy, full-battened sails stemmed from four thousand years of civilisation, which had fortunately so far largely avoided the internal combustion engine. These thoughts were driven out of my head when it became necessary to shorten sail. Lee took the helm. I heard her chuckle of merriment when, as I crawled out onto and clung to the bow-sprit to hand the jib, I was plunged into the heart of one of the monsoon waves over which the junks rode with ease.

Once out through the pass, our course curved to the right to circle the island, the wind came ever freer and we could relax and talk. The moon was down and, on the dark south and east coasts of the island, the sky was ablaze with stars which reflected sparks off the mica facets in the rocks close to starboard; the stern wave curled and broke in phosphorescence.

I cannot remember how we got onto the subject of religion. In my experience it had been encompassed by an attitude of outward observance, surreptitious barrack-room hilarity, comic clergymen and iconoclastic jokes. I remembered, however, that Tom Farr displayed a wide knowledge of comparative religion, the three great monotheisms and their relationship to earlier forms of worship.

I think that what led up to the present conversation was some remark which I made about the Buddhist monastery on Lantau Island, now towering darkly on our port side. "Buddha Gautama was," she said, "brought up by his parents, totally enclosed in an enchanted garden, neither to see nor to know anything of poverty, suffering or disease. He was somehow able to look over the enclosing wall and saw an old man, horribly disfigured by illness or accident, half-starved, in rags, barely human. This started him on the track taken by many religions – austerity – certainly in the Catholic church austerity is allowed so long as it is controlled and supervised in monastic orders. Once austerity gets loose, like in Jansenism, it is brought up with a round turn. Spiritually I am a Catholic, I was brought up that way. Without a continuing spiritual discipline I would be lost; mentally I am probably more in tune with dualists, who thought God did not eject Satan but that good and evil were immutable, primeval entities. There were a lot of sects of this nature during the days of

Catholic civil power, Albigense, Cathars, Bogomils, later Dukhobors – they mostly got the chop."

"And what about the Protestants?" I asked.

She laughed, "When I was a child I was told to run past the Protestant church in case the devil came out."

"Well," I said, "my spiritual longings are satisfied by the naval prayer: 'Preserve us from the dangers of the sea and from the violence of the enemy' and so on, and the hymn "For those in peril on the sea", both excellent aids to navigation and seamanship."

"Yes," she said, "and what about war?"

"Oh, they've done away with that."

A darkened fishing sampan loomed suddenly out of the night. I'd not seen her against the rocks and had to make a sudden, avoiding alteration of course.

We surged on with a quartering wind, past Repulse Bay, with a blaze of light from the imposing hotel, where probably a dance band was still playing; past the scattered lights of Aberdeen, such an unlikely name for a Chinese fishing boat harbour. Lee now had the helm; her anticipation of the surge of each wave kept us steady and, although the boat was too heavy to wave-ride, the minimal rudder usage kept us at maximum speed.

I was recalling that some intelligent teacher had given us a course in comparative religion, when spiritual contemplation was scattered by a sharp increase in wind force. I registered the thought that, with a less skilful person at the helm, I would surely reef down and then flashing back to my previous memory, "It's strange how religious people think that all the others' faiths are false."

Lee glanced confidently up at the straining rigging and said, "The various religions are like the different fingers of God. They point the same way."

At that moment, a freak wave hit the quarter. With a full thrust of the tiller, Lee narrowly avoided a crashing gybe, which would have resulted in the wind catching the wrong side of the main sail, and the force of the heavy spars at its head and foot might have caused disaster. My jaw dropped; she laughed, "A Chinese junk's sail would have been no risk, white man no savee." Junks have no standing rigging.

Dawn broke as we rounded up into a narrow channel inside Green Island, just off-shore of Hong Kong. In the shelter of the mountains we were soon becalmed. Tavy Boy came back to life, unwrapping from his cocoon and brewing up some tea before starting the engine. We puttered back to the dockyard, the harbour, as always, early astir.

Elated, light-hearted, happy, I did not notice that I had missed a night's sleep. Lee washed the salt off her face, flawless in the harsh morning light.

Chapter Eleven

The Riding Party

About a week after our night sail, the signalman came into my temporary cabin in the Tamar, a room which still bore the atmosphere of the vessel's previous incarnation as the local prison ship. O'Leary's deeply tanned face wore an impassive look intended to give the impression that he had not read the enclosed note which he proffered.

"I have the loan of two ponies. Why don't we ride out on Wednesday afternoon? The Mafoo (Chinese groom) will bring them to my flat at 1500." She had not bothered to sign it, nor asked me to lunch. I would not have missed the appointment even had war broken out and guessed that the note needed no reply unless something had detained me – like death.

There seemed to be nothing incongruous in the scene of the beautifully accoutred Chinese groom of a wealthy merchant prince holding two shaggy but well-tended Mongolian ponies standing in a busy street, swishing their tails and, in their excitement, depositing piles of dung to divert the constant stream of clip-clopping pedestrians. It is easy to mount these small animals but Lee seemed to float into the saddle and immediately became a part of her mount.

We rode through a diminishing stream of people towards the clear-cut skyline of the Kowloon Hills, which shielded the little colony from the menacing spaces beyond, where a vast train of waves of history have broken leaving little imprint on the enduring Chinese, the immortal peasants.

Lee replied to my admiration of her riding poise. "Where I grew up it was a tradition to ride before you could talk. The baby was strapped into a saddle basket, until its little nappy-widened crotch could get astride a saddle." She patted her pony's neck. "These are the descendants of Genghis Khan's cavalry mounts; he and his grandchildren very nearly conquered the world with them. But for two chance occurrences they would have subdued the whole continental mass from Europe to Japan." Answering my eager, questioning glance, she continued, "The chief Khan died back home in Central Asia as the armies were poised to take west Europe; the Khans by their immutable custom had to return home to elect the new chief, the wave had spent."

"And Japan?" I questioned.

"Kublai Khan, the Mongol Emperor of China, mounted a powerful invasion force which could have taken out Japan; a typhoon scattered the fleet – it happened twice – and the attempt was not repeated; something similar happened to the Spanish Armada."

After a short trot to clear the city, Lee mused about the "if onlys" of history. "It might have been tidier, a well-disciplined empire across Eurasia. In those days, it was said that a fair maid with a bag of gold could journey from Samarkand to Peking without fear of molestation and, if the Spanish Armada had made for Ireland, upwind of their enemy, we would all speak Spanish and be Catholics."

At this moment two things became clear to me: firstly that I was hopelessly in love, a situation which I had been firmly convinced would be impossible and secondly, that I never tired of listening to Lee's talk whether probing history or the qualities of local equines.

"Scott took these animals to the Antarctic. No other horses could have stood it, but there was no grass or hay down there. Amundsen took dogs. They could eat each other, as the loads got lighter, and he took a lot of dried fruit. Scott's lot died of scurvy."

I could not stop looking at her and I suppose wondering to what extent she was Chinese. There was a very slight fold at the eyelid, which gives to the races, which stem from the central Asian heartland, an appearance of slit eyes. It is said to have been developed as a natural selection process for protection against the windy dust-laden atmosphere of Mongolia but gives rise to a myth of withdrawn inscrutability and immunity to pain. Her complexion without cosmetics radiated a glow of perfect health, which never altered whether she had been immersed in some stuffy den of learning or was in vigorous activity, out-of-doors, in the bright autumn sun of the China coast. I also recalled with a jolt the fact that I had, without conscious effort or resolution, stopped my visits to the brothels of Happy Valley and that my loutish lust was contained by contact with an exceptionally bright mind, informed on a wide variety of subjects, capable of original thought, unbound by fixed ideas. When she gave an opinion it was not entrenched. "There is so much random factor in the universe" was her general qualification. I thought I had met the ultimate intelligence in Tom Farr but here was something different. If, in the past, someone had suggested that I could transfer my love of a woman from her body to her mind, I would have made some ridiculous, coarse disclaimer.

We wound up bridle paths into the hills among the scrub, still leafless from the frightful winds of the typhoon. Lee talked on about the disaster to Kublai Khan's fleet. "The Chinese word means great wind but the Japanese called their saviour 'The Divine Wind'." A small cloud passed across the sun and the sweat was cold on my back.

We talked about Ireland, of whose history I had heard conflicting accounts from English Imperialists and an old Irish servant of my aunt, my surrogate mother. Bridget combined an affection for our family with an abiding hatred of Britain as an entity. "They misgoverned us for eight hundred years – persecuted the Catholics – and caused the potato famine." All this is in her lilting Cork brogue, so similar to the Welsh that it rang true and familiar.

Lee was wholeheartedly Irish but, of course, far less simplistic than Bridget, whose views I recounted.

"No, of course it's nonsense; the Normans came to Ireland just over a hundred years after they conquered England and then established a Norman hegemony: the Norman lords became more Irish than the Irish, fought among themselves, against the Irish chiefs and the King of England. The English held a small enclave with a ring of forts round Dublin, the Pale. All were then Catholic. Later the two countries became embroiled in the religious wars after the Reformation."

She looked up at the sky and made a switch of thought train, "Have you ever noticed that western European religion is climatic? There is a weaving, near-latitudinal line, south of which people are Catholic, north lie the Protestants. The line curves up to embrace South and West Ireland, where the North Atlantic current brings warm water and weather from the Gulf Stream."

We stopped for a while, adjusting stirrup leathers, and I muttered about a Protestant God wearing an overcoat.

Lee switched back to Ireland. "The frightful misgovernment started with the Act of Union of 1801, which removed the Irish Parliament from Dublin to a minority in Westminster, the failure to follow Gladstone's moves towards Home Rule. Also Redmond should have demanded independence in 1914, in return for Irish involvement in the German war. Above all was the foolishness in shooting the leaders of the 1916 rebellion." For a change Lee spoke with such feeling that she laid down attitudes – but then quickly changed back to fantasy and the random factor. "It might have been prevented if Strongbow the Conqueror had been made Norman king with a separate monarchy." Then she considered a moment and continued, "No, the Reformation would have led to a more horrible war."

We paused at a bend in the track to look down on to and across the busy harbour swarming with small craft. A fish-holding barge, flooded to its gunwale and swarming with live fish, was being towed alongside the hotel landing jetty, where the vigorous, darting, silver captives flashed in the sun, as they were scooped out alive, fresh for the tables of affluent diners. The same food chain as for the sharks.

I ruffled my pony's mane and said, "I wonder if they have a race memory of Genghis Khan and Falcon Scott?" – a remark of egregious futility.

This was disconnected by Lee's next remark, which rang to me like a knell. "I wish it could always be autumn in Hong Kong but I must leave in a few weeks. I have a stint coming up in the Massachusetts Institute of Technology, in USA."

When we returned, the mafoo was waiting patiently at the door of Lee's flat and he led the ponies away. Their echoing hoof beats sounded a note of disaster. I had then to return to some dreary duty knowing that I would lose my new-found love in a short space of time.

To go away is to die a little. To part from a focus of love is to die a lot.

Chapter Twelve

Nemesis

Tom and Simon returned from their expedition, with tales of a warlord retreating from gunboat diplomacy and their narrow escape from the typhoon's recurving path. I enjoyed their company less than before and more as a counter-irritant to the deepening despair which ground in my vitals like a fatal disease. I understood how people became terminally ill from cancers which are in the mind or, perhaps, from that part of the mind which is controlled by the spirit.

A high-powered party was to be given by God knows what establishment in a hotel called the "Gloucester Buildings", which combined a flashy welcoming front with a sedate background. The name conjured up the image of council houses in outer London. I normally never went to this sort of thing but tagged along with Simon and Tom. I had managed to get in a fair amount of free drink, before, across a sea of flushed faces and through a mist of cigarette smoke, I saw Lee, surrounded by attentive, attendant, masterful middle-aged men of consequence.

One of them stood out from the others in a reverse situation, a young face with dark hair and handsome features, too pretty for a male. One moment he was at the inner circle; then he quickly faded away.

This was the first time I had encountered Lee in an indoor, social milieu ashore and, I reflected gloomily, probably the last. I stopped gulping drinks and carefully planned my movements, with the object of cutting in at a vital moment when the party started to dissipate. I had little hope but much surprise when my ploy succeeded. "Let's go for a walk," said Lee, "I've had quite enough to eat with all that small chow," (the background munch of a cocktail party for which the naval term was turkey turd and which was frequently made a cheap substitute for dinner). We walked through the streets of the European town, the rickshaw traffic thinning out and with few pedestrians until we reached Wan Chai, the Chinese quarter, acrid and timeless, musical with the clopping of tuned foot clogs; the roof ridges turned up at the bottom to obstruct or prevent the climbing of devils. Banners hung everywhere with Chinese characters, which might have been advertisements but hung like overhead literature. In those days one expected to walk the cities of the world unthreatened. Pax Britannica overlaid the civil as well as the military. Predominantly Cantonese faces passed by in eager discussion and there was a sprinkling of outlanders from all over China, big raw-boned northerners and others from all over Asia. Indian shopkeepers and Arab traders jostled among the thronging Chinese. I walked in a trance of present happiness and future emptiness. We talked a little, perhaps about the party, the return of Simon and Tom. I dimly realised that Lee and Simon were related.

I stopped suddenly to bend down and retie a shoelace. Lee walked on a few yards ahead of me. I glanced up and a light inside a shop flashing on a blade drew my gaze towards a figure crouching in a dark doorway. I gave a fearful shout of warning to Lee and, even as the figure straightened and sprung towards her, she ducked. The speed of movements was too fast for my eye to follow. The armed, black-clad assailant launched himself at her and, obviously impelled and diverted by her trained movements, flew over her shoulder to land with a frightful thump, winded, at my feet, the knife still grasped.

I jumped on his wrist and heard the bone crack but there was no cry, groan or whimper. Then, with amazing recovery, the prone figure rose off the ground and hurtled off into the night with a strange, barking cry. It sounded like 'Minjer' and meant nothing to me. The knife had disappeared; it might have been recovered by his sound hand. I turned towards Lee, who still in a crouch had a knife in her hand. It had a half-moon blade, something like a Ghurka's knife. It was actually a large Bowie but whence had it appeared?

As she straightened up and I started to recover my wits, I saw that she was returning the knife through a bottomless pocket in her skirt. The knife must have rested in a sheath strapped to her thigh. Great Heavens she went armed through life!

"Someone wanted you dead," I said, shakily.

"Yes," she replied, "but it was a clumsy attempt, perhaps more of a threat."

It had looked real enough to me. Lee did not thank me for my warning cry as she had for shooting the tiger poised over her. She said, casually, as we walked away, "Bob, I want you to do something for me. Please mention this incident to nobody." At that time I would have cut out my tongue for her. Later, as we strolled home, she said in some sort of explanation:

"I have had a very intensive course in self-defence disciplines. I was once threatened by some silly family feud; it will blow over."

I was too shattered by the thought of our imminent parting to consider the lameness of this tale. Two weeks later she walked out of my life. It was some months before I returned to Happy Valley.

I spent the next few years superficially active, groping about in submarines, around the periphery of the British Empire that was being sucked into a war, which was to cause its premature, tragic dismemberment.

Within myself I had fallen into a well of despair which, however, was made less bleak by a later heart-warming, brief encounter.

Chapter Thirteen
Abyssinia and Beyond

From the time of its first inception, the submarine was anathema to the British Naval Establishment. Those in high command had sufficient vision to realise that these small, comparatively cheap craft would threaten to neutralise the power of their great battle fleets: further, if rules were broken and merchant vessels attacked, the lifelines of the Island Homeland could be severed. In those days British agriculture could not produce enough to feed its fast growing population. Submarines were hidden underwater, unseen and unfair. Thus our own submarine service grew up disliked, distrusted and under-funded. This made, of course, for intense camaraderie within the submarine family, a close touch between officers and men and a disregard for any regulations which might be flouted with impunity.

Wisely, however, it was decided that submarine officers should, during their careers afloat, spend two periods, each of about eighteen months, in the general service, in order to readjust themselves to the surface navy.

In the mid 1930s I was coming up for my first period of general service. I looked forward, with considerable apprehension to the loss of my submarine pay, six shillings a day, and to entering an alien world. Fortunately, I was saved at the last moment by Mussolini, who invaded Abyssinia.

In what later proved to be futile sabre rattling, the British Empire mustered a great fleet at Alexandria. Note well, at this point, that the main fleet base at Malta, close to Italy, was considered too vulnerable for it to accommodate the fleet, except for some submarines: a few of these were sent in rotation to Alexandria to exercise with the fleet. My appointment to some grand battleship was cancelled and I was ordered to join a submarine as second-in-command to relieve an officer who had suffered serious injury while loading torpedoes.

I was flown out from England to Alexandria with other passengers, in a Sunderland flying boat, the splendid airborne workhorse of those days. The pilot manoeuvred skilfully into the crowded harbour but alighted with too much speed and too close to the jetty. I saw an early death approaching very fast and then receding, as the pilot gunned both engines on one side and, with full rudder, completed an about turn. I wondered had he planned this, as I stepped shakily into the launch, which took me to the cruiser, alongside which lay my new home.

I knew personally all the other officers and quite a few of the crew of the submarine but their characters are not relevant to this story, except that its Commander Officer, like Fred Mailing in China, drank heavily. I liked him personally and had confidence that he could perform his peacetime duties satisfactorily but a shiver ran down my spine when I contemplated the fact that war might ensue. I did not think that we would survive one patrol against any hot opposition.

I thrust these forebodings into the back of my mind when I discovered that Tom Farr was serving in another submarine berthed alongside us.

The cruiser was one of the "County" class, of ten thousand tons displacement, armed with high elevating 8 inch guns. She had big freeboard and looked more like a liner than a warship. She was to stand in for our non-existent depot ship and made us free of her quarters with friendly hospitality. With enormous pleasure and anticipation I met Tom Farr in the Wardroom Officers' Mess before lunch. Tom's face lit up with his usual kindly grin of welcome. "Come down into our boat for a drink, Bob. There is too much of a crowd here."

As we descended the forehatch ladder into the submarine, I experienced the feeling of reassurance, with which one is enfolded on returning to a secure family home.

We sat in the tiny wardroom and, to my surprise, Tom produced a small unlabelled bottle from a locker. He unscrewed the top and I immediately smelled the rich aroma of Navy rum. "Good God, Tom, have you been purloining the sailors' grog ration?"

Tom grinned, "My coxswain is a teetotaller but, instead of drawing his cash allowance he draws his tot, a useful bribe for favours in depot ships and dockyards. The sail-maker of this cruiser is making us some natty curtains. Every now and then, if I don't look too well, the coxswain says, 'You better have my tot, sir'. I'm not much of a drinker, we'll halve it.'

We discussed for a while the practical aspects of using the cruiser as a temporary depot ship, inadequate but friendly. I sipped the strong liquid, the best Jamaica rum, which I had always considered to be, together with the officers' duty-free booze and tobacco, a substitute for adequate pay. That way Britannia always had her navy on the cheap.

We gossiped happily, catching up on our separation and musing over the activities of those whom we knew. I took another sip of the rum and with a quizzical look at Tom I asked, "Do you think there will be a war?"

"Not a hope," he replied confidently. "The League of Nations won't face up, our fleet is not geared for an anti-aircraft struggle. The Ethiops will lose their ancient independence; they cannot stand against modern armaments."

"Well, I am relieved. I think my skipper is a wino and I don't fancy sailing off to war with him, so let's enjoy a not-too-uneasy peace."

Tom's expression brightened. "I've kept the best news for the last," he paused, "Simon is on the staff of a flag officer here and, just down from Cairo where she has been staying with the British High Commissioner, is, guess who, your old flame from Hong Kong."

I was flabbergasted. This could only be Lee O'Connor, whom I believed to have vanished forever, I had no idea that Tom had knowledge of our friendship.

I gave him an incredulous glance, perhaps with raised eyebrows. Tom paused to let my unspoken query sink in.

"Everyone knew everything that went on in Hong Kong; your close friendship sent reverberations round the Colony and, of course, I met her. I used to spend quite a lot of time in the University; had access to the library and so on."

I felt a stab of ridiculous jealousy. Tom was on her mental level. He continued, "Even better, Simon has organised a gorgeous Sunday outing, the day after tomorrow. A forenoon swimming at Sidi Bishr, where the northerly wind kicks up a sea and one can ride the breakers for hundreds of yards into the beach on bellyboards, like we used to in Big Wave Bay in Hong Kong, then a round of golf in the afternoon at Smouha. He is bringing Lee."

"What about transport, do the trams go all the way?"

"Staff officer plus heir-to-peerage equals motor car; Simon has laid on naval transport."

I recalled that all four of us played good, medium-handicap golf. I had brought my clubs in the 'Sunderland'. Simon would have his own. Tom, who had once worked as a caddy, could borrow a set from one of the cruiser's officers, plus another set for Lee.

I finished my half tot and rose. "Well, I have a day and a half to settle into my boat, there will be plenty to do. I expect the chap I am relieving did most of his work in the 'Femina' nightclub. I hope you are right about no war."

"Spot on," said Tom and saw me over the side.

I spent the afternoon going through my boat with a fine toothcomb, in company with the engineer officer, who was obviously right on top of his job. Thank God the machinery worked properly; my worry factor dropped a few points.

Later in the evening I met Tom for a drink in the cruiser's spacious wardroom mess. I put out some feelers about the coming Sunday outing. "I suppose Simon and Lee know one another?"

Tom look startled at my ignorance.

"They are related; everyone is in Ireland. They are related to everyone back to the High King's daughter, who married 'Strongbow', the Norman Conqueror; the only thing is she is a Catholic and he is a Protestant; all Protestants go to Hell."

I reflected that my knowledge of Ireland was less than that of China; that I had never seen Lee in a bathing suit before, that I would abandon my intention to pick up a girl in the "Femina" and I would spend all Saturday morning acquainting myself with the submarine's crew and the rest of the day going through the books.

Sunday dawned clear; it must have been early in the year but, in the sunshine, it was warm enough to swim.

Tom and I hired a felucca, rigged with the beautiful, single, loose-footed lateen mainsail and long yard down to the stemhead, which had suited these waters since the Pharaohs and taken the Arab traders to Africa and the Far East. (It is a splendid rig to windward; but for ease of handling give me Sampan Mary's fully-battened sail.) So we sailed ashore.

We scudded across the harbour threading between warships from all over the British Empire, their crews mustering for Sunday divisions and church, which we had managed to escape with some trumped up excuse and by the general ability of submariners to avoid protocol. I don't think that my new Commanding Officer realised that I had arrived. I had reported to him some time after the bar had opened.

There was a smart car waiting on the jetty, an immaculate Royal Marine driver at the wheel: my heart missed two beats. Lee, dressed in a bush shirt and khaki slacks, bare-headed, hair lifting in the breeze, was standing beside the car. Simon was beside her, pointing out the various warships.

Was it then perhaps that a niggling thought occurred to me? Had Simon a stronger tie with Lee than cousinly affection. I had discovered, from experience of a parallel case, that homosexuals of Simon's type can be sexually attracted to girls who are exceptionally gifted physically, mentally or, perhaps, with a strikingly outgoing personality. I shook this out of my mind. There was nothing doing. Lee would never become the Countess of Mountbriach in a distant bog; the whole world lay at her feet.

Lee and I greeted one another with happy accord. I was assailed by none of the clumsy shyness and gaucherie to which I was usually prone. We slipped straight back into the friendly, uncomplicated happiness, which I thought to have left forever in Hong Kong.

We drove to Sidi Bishr chatting happily between the four of us. Lee sat beside the impassive chauffeur. No more ill-natured thoughts assailed my mind. My cup of contentment was full. As if to top it up, Simon said, "I got the Admiral's steward to pack up a picnic with a thermos of chilled wine; we will have a jolly lunch."

There were bathing huts for changing and I realised that I would have to exert mental control when Lee appeared in a swimsuit. I was glad of the coolness of the water.

I don't know if modern surfing had been invented at that time; nowadays, standing up on specially designed boards to ride huge ocean rollers is an ultimate test of skill and balance. Riding the breakers face down in the waves on a random-selected short piece of plank, perhaps the floorboards of a car, was exhilarating for amateur innovators: skill was needed to control the split second, which would give you a ride, to select the wave, which would bring you right up to the shore, to mount the forward rolling crest at the right angle and to avoid being painfully dumped nose downwards into the sand. We all became proficient after about half-an-hour. We were young, tireless and warmed by exertion.

After we had towelled and dressed, the driver brought down the picnic basket. There were thinly-cut, chicken salad sandwiches and some fruit, two thermoses of fine French white wine, decanted from chilled bottles, and a thermos of hot Turkish coffee with flag officers' glass and chinaware. The driver preferred more solid fare and munched in the car. Simon said, "I offered him a swim but he thought it unbecoming to his station."

Lee put a comb through her hair and shook it in the sun and wind, free of straggly tangles, black, red undershooting showing momentarily.

I felt entirely relaxed and happy, inapprehensive about the future, at peace with myself in company with my close friends and the woman, who, I was certain was the only one I would ever love. They were all people who went through life without ever taking umbrage or becoming miffed; faults to which I was frequently prone. The cool wine, particularly delicious in retrospective comparison with the rough stuff to which I was accustomed, encouraged nostalgia. Simon had finished his lunch and was sipping wine, an unfamiliar, veiled expression on his face. He looked across the sparkling waves and, without ado, started to soliloquise about the west of Ireland.

"My happiest childhood memory is of seeing a toggle of swans coming into an enclosed sea inlet and seeking shelter from threatening weather on the coast." He paused entranced by the mental picture.

> 'All's changed since I, hearing at twilight,
> The first time on this shore,
> The bell-beat of their wings above my head,
> Trod with a lighter tread.'

Then, without pausing, he continued "The magic quality lies in the fast changing light; the weather patterns come in off the sea with startling suddenness, free of land friction or hill forms; an oceanic climate in a coastal setting of unbelievable, unspoilt beauty, the people mostly primitively rural and poor; those that are not forced to emigrate are happy, healthy and friendly."

Lee shook her head as though clearing a dream. "If you go to a party of affluent strangers in England, they mostly appear to dislike you. They cannot really dislike you because they don't know you; in Ireland, at a gathering of people of any class, they all appear to like you."

Tom, who had once walked along the border of Northern Ireland, murmured, "Yes, even if they hate you and would like to shoot you, they still appear to like you."

"True Christianity," I said and wished at that second I'd left it unsaid. "Thou shall love thy neighbour as thyself, even if thou wantest to shoot him."

The conversation had taken a wrong turn and, eating the delicious, insubstantial sandwiches, we started to discuss the local political impasse of which we were the centre.

I queried Simon about the possibility of force being used and, at the same time, an idea arose in my mind that we should not discuss such things in front of Lee, a civilian, but I immediately dismissed the thought; I recalled her saying that she was to dine with the Commander-in-Chief that evening and that she had been staying with the British High Commissioner in Cairo. She was part of the Establishment of Empire. Nonetheless, I was surprised when Simon remarked bluntly, "The Commander-in-Chief does not consider that the fleet is adequately protected against the Italian modernised airforce."

We clinked our glasses in a toast and then drank the steaming Turkish coffee out of eggshell thin cups. I poured a libation of coffee grounds from the thermos into the sand, we packed up the picnic and drove off through the crowded streets, swerving past trotting gharries and clanking trams to the golf club at Smouha.

We were immediately welcomed by a bevy of prospective caddies in Egyptian dress, which looked like a colourful night-shirt but was eminently practical in hot weather; as the body warmed the atmosphere around it, an ascending column of air rose and cooled the wearer.

Simon chose three whom he knew. Tom insisted on carrying his own clubs which caused some discomfiture, the Egyptian fellahin being poor to the border of starvation. However Tom was adamant. "This was my profession," he said. It was a reaction to an ingrained habit of enforced parsimony.

We decided to play a foursome, two against two, rather than the slow unwieldy four ball. Somehow I drew Lee for my partner. I liked to try to hit the ball a long way. Lee had uncanny accuracy, with constant practice she could have been a scratch player, but I realised that we would be hard put to beat Tom's expertise, generated by his experience as a caddy, allied to Simon's steady performance.

As we walked over the springy turf of the golf course, I trod not so much with a lighter tread, more as though on clouds. Between our alternate shots Lee and I chatted happily about our lives, as though we had never separated. Impelled by Simon's emotional sally at lunch, I questioned her about her feelings for Irish nationalism. "No," she said, quietly but definitely, "it's largely rooted in fantasy and falsified history. There would eventually have been sufficient independence if the parliament had been kept in Dublin in 1801. Yeats, who wrote the lovely 'swan' poem that Simon quoted at lunch, said of the 1916 rebellion 'a terrible beauty was born'. I don't think it was, I'm not one for violence."

There flashed before my eyes an earlier scene in Wanchai, when a dark-clad assailant flew over her shoulder and a knife appeared in her hand from nowhere. Well, self-defence is an inalienable right.

"And Simon," I asked.

"Simon does live in a Celtic twilight."

She would go no further than this. The mental picture of an Irish nationalist sitting close beside the admirals, flickered momentarily and disappeared.

We all played above our normal form, the caddies capered admiringly; they were captivated by Lee speaking colloquial Arabic. The game passed like a dream, which I would have wished to continue indefinitely; we were all square on the eighteenth green and Lee sank the winning putt from quite a distance, a fact which made me absurdly happy. We tipped the caddies generously (their hashish ration) and took long, cool drinks onto the club verandah. I must have had a premonition of doom; perhaps I had picked up some hints or thought waves during the match.

Lee explained that she was only stopping in Alexandria for the Commander-in-Chief's dinner party, that night, (it was a most unusual occasion for a Sunday) to host the visit of some American big shot who was en route for Cairo. Lee was to accompany him next day as bear-leader in the political, social and university worlds. I must have emitted some gloomy vibrations. Lee suddenly turned her face towards me and, without speaking, glanced at me with a look which I had never seen before; it was the unmistakable expression of affection, something which I had to save up and treasure. I returned silent to my gin and tonic, while the others discussed the Stepped Pyramid of Zoser and the quality of our golf. When I came to again I resurrected the Irish dispute:

"Simon, do you think that Ireland should have been part of the United Kingdom?"

"Not on your nelly." He was firm but not aggressive. "Ireland should be an independent united nation; OK, the Northern Protestants are Scottish settlers but they are simply re-entered, ancient Irish Celts. The Celts swept up from the south, displacing the Picts, and then settled in Scotland: different religion, colder climate; but they are more similar than say a Geordie and a person from Wessex."

I thought it better not to pursue the matter further. It was simple, Simon was an ardent Irish Nationalist, Lee was an Imperialist. We drove Lee to someone's flat to change for the C-in-C's dinner. I put on a brave face or so I thought; Tom and I returned to our ship.

The personalities of my new submarine's crew have no bearing on this tale. The remainder of the Abyssinian fiasco is history; the unopposed aggression, which had been started by the Japanese in Manchuria, was sweeping forward unchecked. The submarines returned to Malta, where I explored the Strada Streta, (a red-light district since the rule of the Knights of St John), but I had scant enthusiasm for these adventures. After a decent pause we returned to England, at the time when the great ruthless dictatorships, Germany and Russia, soon to be leagued against us, were just about to try out their weapons on opposite sides in the erupting Spanish Civil War. As we pushed slowly up the coast of Portugal, a Spanish warship passed us, steaming southward at high speed. There was a great plume of black smoke from her funnels. The engineer officer was on the bridge. "Bad stoking," he said scornfully. Later I was told that the crew had mutinied and taken over the ship to join the communists and were then burning the officers in the boilers – bad stoking, indeed.

I was looking forward to my return home. There were new submarines being built. I would soon be posted to my qualifying course for Submarine Commanding Officer. This was the limit of my ambition. I had no desire for promotion to high rank nor did I think that I had a chance of this. As far as I was concerned, the submarine commanding officer was the head of my profession. After that, I would retire on half pay or whatever it was and live a life of adventure.

The adventure came sooner than I expected and, by this time, I had command of an operational submarine.

Chapter Fourteen
War 1939

We sat, four men, around the table, in a small compartment, ringed with pipes, valves, electric leads and switches. All this machinery was carefully marked and maintained, all having a meaningful purpose to preserve our own lives or a deadly purpose to destroy the lives of others. We were girt within our own little world, shut off from the rest of mankind. Our little world was a submarine, in the disputed North Sea, in 1939. We had existed and fought wholly together for many months. Outsiders often posed the question, "Don't you get on one another's nerves?" No, we had got *off* one another's nerves into one another's personalities. It was like an old-settled marriage.

The boat rocked slowly and pumped lethargically up and down, in time to the swell generated by the screaming tempest above us, which was blowing the top of the sea toward Europe. We drank our tea and shook the afternoon sleep from our eyes. Opposite to me sat Tom Farr, now our first lieutenant, his thin, drawn features and anatomy, precise mouth and glance was the outward reflection of his keen mind and deep intelligence. Without any robustness or ordinary powers of leadership, he ran the boat in splendid fashion, simply because he could solve most problems, human or technical with clear, easy brainpower. The men liked this; they not only knew where they were, they knew they were right. I did not think that Tom's physique could stand up for very long to the infernal racket of increasing action, but his unathletic make-up seemed to make him less dependent on oxygen and movement, which our daily life lacked. How much more it was to lack, in the long summer days which were to come, I was dimly beginning to realise.

On my right, sucking in his breath in vexation at not being able to smoke, was Jack Lamb, Warrant Engineer Officer, small, dark and sharp he was in love with his profession, the main engines and his recently wed, lovely wife in Birmingham whom, with realistic fatalism, he did not expect to live to enjoy for very long. He had just finished a diatribe on our conditions, "Of course I'd never have got married if I'd known this lot was coming."

"But good heavens, Chief," said Tom, "why couldn't you see it coming? I thought everyone did, except our rulers."

"Well, I didn't have time to read the papers," said the Chief Engineer. "Pass the jam, Number One. I suppose it's blackberry and apple again. Why don't you get that bloody pusser in the depot ship to use his imagination?"

"Too much worry about bodily needs," said Tom, sipping his tea reflectively. "The body is only a springboard for the mind; it's no good fussing about the tension of the springboard if the diver is rotten."

This brought Frank Girling on my left out of his trance, "Just as long as the body is good enough for a nice lot of shack shack, when we get back to harbour, but will it be with all these sawdust biscuits and tinned food?" Frank was a Royal Naval Reserve lieutenant, dark and craggy, he had the look of a gypsy prize-fighter: he had served in all manner of merchant ships including a spell in sail and a time in an Antarctic whaler. He navigated to perfection, had no cares and lived for women.

The curtain across the corridor parted and in looked the red, merry face of Bill Frazer, the Royal Naval Volunteer Reserve third hand. Bill should have been a regular sailor; he came of the Samurai class of England, a line of Norman colonels and colonial administrators. His father, realising that his was a dying class, had put him in the city to revive the family fortunes; all that Bill earned he had spent on sailing yachts and that experience of the sea had netted him into this unreal, underwater hide-and-seek.

"I had to take her down to eighty feet, sir," he said, ruefully. "The planesmen can't hold sixty feet in this storm swell."

"Well you must raise the asdic dome," I replied. "There are only fourteen feet under our keel now, if you lose depth you will rub it off." He scratched his head in dismay. "Then, sir, we can neither see nor hear. We might as well..." Chief finished off the comforting family joke, "Stick around Piccadilly Underground."

I was now considering the next problem. We had to rise to a shallow depth to put our wireless aerial in a position to receive the routine four-hourly broadcast from Headquarters. We could barely hold this depth in the crashing waves above; the boat tended to break surface like a porpoise. Further, the easiest course for our depth-keeping planesmen, beam on to the swell, was not the easiest course for the wireless waves to be trapped in an aerial. We would have to compromise; a nightmare of conflict between the sweating planesmen and the eagerly listening radio operator. Every increase in speed to aid the forward and after hydroplanes, which controlled our depth-keeping, meant a drain on precious battery power.

I called the crew to diving stations; only the full skill of everyone could hold the required depth in this storm.

I stood in the control room between the periscopes. Tom hanging from his steadying arms, which clutched overhead pipes, tried to balance the boat's trim, speed, battery power and plane control against the sickening inertial surges of wave motion, incalculable lift and drop. Max Pell, the huge, imperturbable coxswain swung the big, brass wheel between his shoulders, controlling our angle while we slowly climbed up to forty-five feet. I watched the play of muscle and wheel and my mind flung back many years in time. A newly-joined, ignorant, unseaman-like junior officer, my first trip in a submarine, down the Formosa Channel off the China coast in a heavy following sea; three of us were down on the casing deck securing some loose fitting; a curling wave top caught and swept me, unprepared. I knocked my head on the saddle tanks just before a great sea took me. Max, champion swimmer of the China Fleet, not heeding to peel off his jacket, leapt out and caught me up and somehow swam us both back, as the submarine swung round and stopped upwind of us. Since this incident, Max had a fatherly love for me, which was somehow not disturbed now that I was the father figure.

I did not halt our upward drive to listen out on our asdic; no trawlers would be around above us in the maelstrom; up went the periscope so that I could look every time we, involuntarily, clove the surface of the waters. We struggled with the seesaw motion, trying to anticipate the moments of inertia impelled by the vast, circular movements inside the wave crests. We hung strangely for a time-still, oily fragment of life, while I could look carefully, swinging the periscope round the hate-filled, elemental storm. I saw it then; I'd seen plenty before but not in this helpless position. Dark, shaggy, barnacle-crusted, evilly-horned, a floating mine lay across our path and bows. Instant messages flowed inside me, "Get her down, turn, swing the bows away, don't put the stern into her, will the cable catch us? Too late now to move, we haven't enough way on."

The mine had a little way on her. The surface drift above was greater than that acting on our hull. She was blowing across us but mercifully she did not bob down, no cable hung, no one had seen my jaw drop, so why should I frighten the others?

As the cry from the wireless office signified that the routine message was finished, our crew lost control of the boat and she porpoised. First we broke surface and lay half-awash in the crashing seas, now tearing at the light plating of our casing decks and smashing away plates and gratings, a helpless target for aircraft and, as the sky was clearing of its cloud, I cast an anxious eye round for the prowling, ceaseless patrols. Then speeding and flooding we surged downwards; we failed to catch her and sped down towards the bottom. Scarcely pulling out of the dive, the keel hit the sand with a juddering crash; instantly our tension was dissolved into the healthy fear of disaster and damage, into action and postmortem investigation. Tom, for all his brainpower, had not yet developed the instinctive feel like a pilot flying his machine by the seat of his pants. I had felt the inertial pull; my eyes were on the sky and, by the time I had looked back, it had been too late. Martin Smith, the second coxswain, working the forward planes, was one turn out of phase and fighting against the coxswain's drive with the great stern planes.

Smith, taller even than his senior, Pell, though not so broad, looked like a Viking chief, fair, proud and eagle-eyed. It seemed impolite to upbraid him and indeed he knew his fault. I didn't tell them that, had we broken the surface a little earlier, we would have hit that mine.

All the efforts had not been in vain; we had received our wireless orders and presently decoded, I read "Do not proceed east of line... intense enemy antisubmarine effort here." Later it transpired, three British submarines were lost in that area. Southward there were the fishing grounds so infested with trawlers, some undoubtedly enemy patrols, that there was barely room to turn. There was only one thing for it, we must patrol inside the German minefield; I'd seen many floating mines, the storms had dispersed them.

And so it was, while the storms abated. After one has swept out an area of sea with one's tender skin it seems to get safer.

Some days later, not long after lunch ,I was woken out of my half sleep by the cry "Captain in the control room." I leapt swiftly in one movement, my guts pulling like after one of those deadly pills they gave you at school. "A bunch of trawlers, sir," said Tom, relinquishing the periscope, "in this minefield they are not fishing."

No, by God, they weren't, and how in hell and why, pointing this way? We were a needle in a haystack and had done no harm nor showed ourselves: waiting ambushers should not be ambushed. But there they were, spread out in deadly, expectant array, the net spread for us. A tip up with the periscopes sky searcher revealed the clue, a monster Dornier flying boat was spiralling down from his high vulture perch, where Tom had missed him. He could not see us in this murky, shallow water unless... and, if so, this was it... if that mighty bump on the bottom had opened a leak in an internal fuel tank, a long oil slick could be flagging them home to us. Only one thing to do, turn, beam on to the wind, let the slick blow sideways and zigzag till dusk, keep observation on him until forced deep; these were all my quick trained thoughts.

We got quickly to diving stations and I started to try to weave through a gap in the line. I'd now lost my internal surroundings and concentrated on the outside above with an actor's poker face. I tried to imagine how brave officers rallied their men by walking imperturbably along the firestep with their heads in the bullet stream. One must have a swagger stick, well the periscope handles must do. So they came on, so my periscope bobbed and swung. I always told myself I was only afraid in a specialised claustrophobic war. Later, I had small tastes of other people's wars, in low-flying attack aircraft, shore bombing raids, infantry men's machine gun dread. I found out I was just plain scared. We slipped noiselessly through the nearest gap in our foe line, then the wicked bow spun round towards us. I could see men scurrying round the depth charge throwers. "He is going to stamp on us, Number One," I said. "Take her down." As we reached down for eighty feet, it came. I won't write down the noise, it still frightens me. I looked round at a perfectly organised action repair squad: the auxiliary lights came on out of the pitch dark, a man with a rubber-covered wheelspanner was tightening a hissing leak, another replacing fuses. Chief, with his torch, padded silently towards a disaster point; Martin Smith wrestled the fore hydroplanes in hand drive, thank God for his Viking strength.

I said in a thickish voice, "He bombed the oil slick on our starboard side, continue the zigzag at silent speed."

"Should we speed away now, sir?" said Girling, looking up from his plot.

"Yes, if it was peace with an hour's exercise, but not now, just keep this up, Frank." I willed confidence into my orders. "But you can try to work out the difference between the tidal stream down her and what it is at the surface, then, maybe, we can set a course to throw the oil slick further out."

I knew the enemy had only three more hours of light, that he had no supersonic hunting gear and that he only had a limited supply of depth charges, that he probably couldn't get more help out from home, that he might not want to, feeling cocky at seeing the oil slick. And so it went on and I got into a mental groove of listen and slow dodge, work away till dark and then make for home. I remembered a book by a distinguished army doctor. "Every man has just so much store of fortitude. It differs widely in individuals but everybody has a cracking point somewhere."

Could the store be measured in depth charges? And how many would we score this time? And next time?

I remembered a night in the pub at Sheerness, just as war started; an old timer of 1914 said, "My God I pity you! I know what it's like, day after day, night after night, month in month out for years!" We were both tipsy and I felt valorous and swashbuckling; now I smelt gas from the batteries, not chlorine but acrid and combustive, that must wait, if they would only hold out two more hours. As the winter sky darkened far above us, the pursuit faltered and I made a major slow turn upwind. They blew away from us and we leapt up into the night. The diesels spluttered and we tore home.

Chapter Fifteen

Sailor Ashore

I threw a suitcase into the back of my battered 3-litre Bentley. Tom jumped in beside me, glad of the lift but groaning at the cold, open car in winter. I drove slowly up towards London; if we sped up the breeze froze us and we had no hood.

Tom turned half towards me. "I'm sorry, Bob, I ballsed up that crash down and it nearly finished us."

"We could have played it another way," I said to soothe him. "I might have missed out that routine, conditions weren't possible. We'd have picked up the signals at night. We might even have surfaced, but we wanted to keep the patrol position secret, now it's blown anyway. Tom how would you like to be the German Emperor now?"

Tom said slowly, "We can just about hold his ring but, as you know, if you can bear to know, our sea power is years out-of-date. We don't have the force for far-flung Empire any more. These boats are antiquated sort of Heath Robinson affairs; there isn't the right link between scientific design and weapon requirements: my destroyer chum told me that the sailors chipping paintwork put a hammer through the side." He thought again. "Our air and sea lords have been fighting each other, our engineers and upper deckmen behave like trades unionists. Where is that happy band of brothers that Nelson led?"

"Tom," I said, "you've told me this sort of thing before."

He laughed, "If only someone had told the British people this sort of thing before, that what they should have spent on adequate defences is an infinitesimal portion of what they will have to spend on this war."

"Well," I said, "there is no big sea power against us now. I exclude, of course, those festering trawlers we met."

"No," he said, "not now."

A comradely silence fell between us. I drove on, enjoying the feel of the powerful car on well-nigh deserted roads, with no twinge of conscience about the illicit acquisition of my petrol coupons.

Tom was looking up at the clearing sky, where soon every star would be seen over the blacked-out country. Without embarrassment, he said, "I suppose you will be seeing Caroline."

"Right. I had no idea you knew her."

"She has been the mistress of half the nobility and gentry, as listed in Debrett. But that is backstairs gossip. Also, she is related to Simon."

"Tom," I said, irritably, "are you trying to warn me off?"

Tom laughed, "No. I'm warning you on. I think she is just what you need but I don't think that you should fall in love."

I was silent. There was no possibility of that situation.

It was getting dark as we drove through the East End and, finally, we slid into my favourite place to leave the car and I zipped up the tonneau cover. I told Tom, "Get lost and don't delay me, not for an instant." I hailed a cab and before long, parked my overcoat and suitcase with the pretty hat-check girl at the "Fakers Club". Caroline was at the bar; this was where we had first met, drawn together by our mutual failings: she was a natural nymphomaniac, I in an hysterical, sexual overdrive. She soon shed her "Eagle Squadron" friend and came to me.

Caroline had a lovely figure and a face like a slightly puzzled pixie. Her parents were abroad, governing in a minor way. Her uncle was an earl, which was important in pre-war days, and tokened some background and tradition. I could not understand why she had fallen into living in night clubs or why, above all, she had fallen to me.

"Bobby," she said, "you look more than usually pale and interesting."

"Yes, my gymnastic physique just poisons me when it's not used. I'm short of sleep and oxygen and love."

"Two drinks here and we'll hit the 'Cubano', the band is good and they have that 'Bulls Blood' wine you dote on. I'm tired of protecting myself from insistent airmen."

"And I'm afraid, afraid of losing you; there are too many cowboy film stars around."

More drinks later than I wanted, we moved on, and here I felt on my own ground: we sat at a table, drank wine, thought we might get food sometime and I drank in Caroline and forgot the rest of the room. I hardly noticed the cigarette girl poking her bottom into my left shoulder as she served the next table. I didn't hear the Yank on my right, who was eating soup under my elbow. I did not hear the band going shack, shack shack. I wanted to get right inside Caroline, body and mind. I wanted to hide from my sick fear. I wanted, above all, to get away to bed soon. We danced, if you can call that huddle-muddle dancing. There was no privacy for talk; I began to make excuses to go home. "This underground cave is beginning to smell like my half-fused battery."

She smiled. "Don't discuss the war, someone might report you."

"Well, I've had no fresh air for weeks, let's walk it home."

After a bit, she gave in, rather crossly, and we walked the half mile to her flat. I clung unashamedly. "Have they called you up yet sweetheart? I expected to see you as a female dockyard matey in Chatham."

"I have an Irish passport," she said, coldly.

"Great Scott, I never knew, you a neutral, but how can you be now?"

"There is something wrong with you," she said, irrelevantly. "You don't like people, men are something to fight with, for or against, women are toys or a refuge."

"I cannot see..."

"And, furthermore, you haven't grown up since you left that damn Naval College at seventeen. You are packed too full of King Arthur's knights and middle-class morality."

"Well, I've graduated from Sir Galahad to Sir Lancelot," I said remembering Tom Farr's simile.

"And, furthermore," she said, without pausing to notice my elephantine response, "I hate your old British Empire and I despise you for not having a navy to keep it."

"What do you know of the fleet anyway? Your friends must be indiscreet."

"I have a cousin in it. I grew up with him. Simon Dunbulben." This information gave a bizarre twist to our relationship. I couldn't understand why she blew up. The flat was small, sordid, cosy. The main furnishing was a gramophone and record cabinet and a bed with a broken mattress, which was slung like a hammock.

"What's the matter with this frenzy?" Caroline took my forehead. Halfway through the night, I woke up shouting and pouring sweat. I'd to sponge down and we changed the sheets.

By morning I had dropped through rough sharpness into deep sleep until about ten o'clock. I woke to see Caroline sitting naked at the end of the bed and staring into the gas fire. She turned slowly towards me, as if she had heard me wake. I whispered "You're at the wrong end of the bed, you lovely waif."

"Don't count your blessings too often," she said, but came towards me. I knew then that I could go on patrolling the hostile waters, so long as I did not fall in love with Caroline, which I might well have done, considering our sexual compatibility, were it not for the fact that I was already totally dedicated to someone who never left my thoughts though she might just as well be at the other side of the moon.

At noon we got up and she cooked us brunch of eggs and scraps and we drank hot, sweet tea. I knew I'd got a longer leave than usual as the boat had to be patched up. I let this fact drop slowly. I knew Caroline and I would get on each other's nerves after the flush of wild passion was slaked. I didn't like her dancing with, in particular, a French air liaison officer with polished Breton cheeks.

"Listen," she said, "we'll go to Ireland for a few days and stay with my uncle. Surely you can have a bogus Irish relative and wangle some leave to see the old non-existent dear."

"Very non-existent," I said, "my ancestors were Saxon and Welsh carpetbaggers who followed Cumberland's army into Scotland in 1745. Carpetbaggers always wax rich and marry the locals. I've no Irish in me."

"Well, you come from the Celtic fringe, if you could recall your two hundred year old Welsh accent, I'd pass you as a Cork man."

I pulled back the curtains and looked into the pale, wintry day. A shy shaft of sunlight lit the cobbles of the mews yard. People were about their work. I stood still in time, putting on my uniform, which smelt of diesel fuel; it was my best and was kept in the depot ship, but it stank from being near my working suit.

"We'll go," I said, "as long as there is no enforced virginity: I've heard that you're all Jansenists over there."

"We'll go," she said, "on two conditions: one, no hint of the life that I lead will reach my uncle or the village - they must not be hurt - and this does entail virginity - two, don't put on your Protestant face."

"What do you mean? I haven't been to church since the war started."

"Catholics get rid of their sins in confession at regular intervals - Protestants carry them around for life in a sort of bank balance account against good deeds: it shows in their expressions. Besides they look down on everyone else who is not clean, honest and truthful, such unimportant virtues."

"Are you a Catholic?"

"No," she said, "I'm nothing. I don't mean it humbly, I suppose I'm nearest to a Chinese Taoist; Tao is 'the way', only I've lost the bloody thing."

"Weren't you brought up a Protestant by your parents?"

"My parents were always away. My uncle is an Anglo-Irish ascendancy Protestant. My nurse, who gave me the only love I knew, treated me as a Catholic. Intellectually, I can't accept either. I can't believe in their hells; I can't worship a God, who is presented as a supreme sadist and who invented a method of rendering the human nervous system indestructible for all time, so that it could suffer tortures, which human monsters can only inflict for limited periods."

I had never heard Caroline speak philosophically before, and I had thought theology was taboo. My own moral tissue had been compounded by a clergyman teacher, who paid assiduous attention to bottom whacking, which I connected vaguely with ultimate divine retribution, with a syndrome of boy-scout, public school, naval discipline, truthfulness, loyalty-efficient code, immorality, VD and hellfire, gin, sodomy and the lash, starched white shirts and clean, bright work on Sunday. It was too muddled to clarify into a doctrine. I pushed the memory of my life with the whores of Hong Kong into the background.

The facade, which had been re-erected after I fell in love with Lee, had collapsed under pressure of constant fear and discomfort. If I risked hellfire by sharing Caroline's bed, it was a risk I preferred to the certainty that I did not have the fibre to look forward to a temporal hell without a measure of relief.

I said, "Look at life. The creator gave us a safety valve so that, if pain is intolerable for long, death supervenes. The Greeks invented the myth of the safety valve gagged down, Prometheus bound, his liver pecked by the eagle and always renewed; an invention of cruelty by someone who detested the sight of his victim's escape into death. The clerics hold it as a super birch to keep us good. I don't know if it does or if it increases the potential evil in power maniacs who think 'if God is cruel, why not I?' I've stepped out from under the birch and this tokens a change of thought. Perhaps we are thinking wishfully and push away the thought that we might wake up frying on a griddle."

"Well, darling, you can push the thought away for the next few days, look around you at women who are chaste and in touch with God. There are two hundred bicycles outside the chapel at mass every Sunday. How many would be on your quarterdeck church rigout of capstan bars and buckets, if they weren't marched in? I'm not trying to convert you to anything. I'd like you to see the people I love. Find out what makes them loveable – also a breath of country air would do you no harm."

Chapter Sixteen
The Irish Connection

We walked across the unkempt lawns towards Castle Mountbriach. The Georgian mansion, displaying its classic line against a watery sky, was mouldering in a zareba of trees. There must once have been some good fields but now thistle and ragweed had sprung up wherever reeds and swamps gave place. The whole drainage was choked. Unthinned plantations reached up but were dwarfed by over-mature monsters. The original Norman castle was an ivy-covered ruin.

Caroline walked beside me across the mossy meadows. I had the strange illusion that she had levitated horizontally and lay with her head in the hollow of my shoulder.

"Great heavens. What happens when the old man dies and Simon inherits, will he take this over?"

"On a lieutenant-commander's pay?" she said bitterly. "No, it's dead. The remaining estate workers are old, have cottages which were good by the standards of 1800, pay no rent, grow their own potatoes in a small piece of drained bogsoil, cut their turf free, drag firewood from the unkept woods and get free milk and the pension. Their wages are occasionally paid in whisky. There isn't much whisky left. The next generation won't have it this way. This is the end. Uncle Donald was loved, so it wasn't burnt in the Troubles."

"I'm rather shy at meeting your uncle. Doesn't he hate the middle classes?"

"Of course, he does, but he hides it under a torrent of charm. He has lived among the politest people on earth – for twenty generations."

"Well, I've seen Irish stokers do the most impolite things on a Saturday night run ashore."

"Oh, I don't mean prissy sort of politeness. I mean the important things like not hurting people's feelings, not being glued to truthfulness, not being dull or censorious." We came into a dark hall and I saw what she meant by the end. The old butler bowed and said, "Welcome home, Miss Caroline" and then shook my hand dumbly. I saw that he was crying.

We walked across unswept, parquet floors, through rooms of perfect proportion spoiled by Victorian clutter and hideous trophies of chase and war, anything of artistic merit must have been sold long ago to pay the creeping debts. The old man greeted us in a sanctum of leather, whisky, tobacco, past glory and authority. His splendid sport-forged body, with a replica of Simon's carved Norman face and high colour, could have been any age. He was shaky with high blood pressure, evidently did not like his life and had taken refuge behind the whisky bottle. He couldn't last much longer nor could he be a host or companion to us.

"Welcome, my boy; always glad to see one of your cloth over here. I wonder if you knew my brother, the admiral? Used to play polo in Malta. Got killed in a hunting fall, always took his fences too fast. My son, Simon, must be about your time. Never seem to see him now. Well we will have a look at the trees tomorrow. Caroline will show you the house. I get tired these days." His mind started to wander. Caroline led me away.

After dinner, which was vile and cold, the old man left us quickly, tottering back to his lonely vigil with his only friend. The dusty, torn curtains shut out the night. The big dining table was unused; a small nursery table had been drawn up close to the flickering turf fire.

Caroline pushed the decanter to me. "This is the last bottle of vintage port. Luckily I know how to decant and it's not faded. Uncle Don drinks whisky. You and I are the only people to appreciate it."

"I'm here for a few days. I won't find out much about things or people, the Irish people, why you love them, why they'd detest your way of life, why, above all, you detest the British Empire, with which your family has concerned itself for some time. I know what makes you tick in a nightclub, but not here."

"It's not the British Empire, it's the London Empire, as surely as was Rome's of that city. The Norman oligarchy still rule, sitting on the city bullion sacks. It's defended by the navy and policed by Celtic and Indian mercenaries. It has only one excuse for existence, to keep the major peace. It hasn't done this; it hasn't done it twice now; that's too often. I don't understand the maritime technicalities of failure, though I learnt a bit from Simon. I dimly realise the unbalance of the two Englands, the ins and the outs. I do understand how and what an insecure, political base was made here in this island."

"Well, I can tell you two short maritime technicalities." I was now into my third glass of port which, unlike naval port, didn't feel like swallowing a tom cat backwards.

"Firstly, in the days of sail, England, being upwind, was very hard for the European navies to assault. They had to beat up to windward. It would have been fatal for England had they secured a base in this island upwind. Secondly, nowadays all the supplies to Britain from the New World come round this island; the focal points lie right under your shores. If the Germans' submarine campaign becomes effective, we might lose this war without Irish bases."

"Well, politically, you had two choices, either exterminate the inhabitants like Ghengis Khan, and even Cromwell did not manage that, or treat them like human beings. The mistake has been made for too long. Not only was the home base insecure but millions of Irish Americans hate the guts of the London Empire. Most of them hardly know why, but many are now rising to top posts in their own country."

I realised that Caroline was politically swayed by her emotions.

"Well, you've told me your hate thing. Tell me the love part. I wanted to know the springs of her love for the local people. Was it a maudlin, lady bountiful, village-patronising sympathy?

But this touched too deeply. She looked lost and said, "I had a mother somewhere, Mother Ireland perhaps. Soon I'll start talking psychiatric twaddle. Why don't you love, Bobby? You love your crew, an entity. You'll never love a person. "

"I was taught young that my trade shouldn't marry, like paupers can't; we erect shells around us, substitutes, some like gin, some efficiency. I sort of flop on my crew and officers; I don't think they like it much, they'd rather be led or bullied. Well, you seem to be in love with a peasant image."

We talked our way down the past as I drank most of the decanter and talked our way out of passion. In my bedroom the unclipped ivy tapped the window.

Next morning, an ancient postman arrived at ten o'clock with a telegram, "Return to duty forthwith." I grumbled, "Great heavens, those repairs were due to take three weeks. What's biting them?" Caroline boiled us eggs and made tea. The old uncle wasn't stirring. After breakfast, I discovered that Simon never came near the place, couldn't stand the dereliction nor his father's drinking. The Irish Land Commission would take the untended fields and the Georgian roof would fall in, the stones would go for road fill and one more building would be struck from the list of Palladio's imitations. Old Lady Mountbriach had bolted with a Scottish Master of Foxhounds, had since been three different peeresses and finished up an uncrowned maharanee in an inebriates' home. Donald Mountbriach gave up hunting, which had been his life, gave up life and just got sozzled.

Next morning, we walked down a potholed road, bordered by dripping trees, to the dilapidated village, which, at 9.30 a.m., showed no sign of stirring. How, I wondered, did the children get to school? The tiny post office was embedded in a dwelling house, from which came no sounds of animation. An ancient post-mistress ground the handle of an unwieldy machine and, after a sharp exchange in Gaelic, was able to connect me to the offices of the shipping company. It would not be possible to cross the Irish Sea for the next two days. "Well," said Caroline, "there will not be time to show you the country or its people but we will have a day out with the hounds. I can borrow a couple of hunters from the doctor and there are boots and hunting clothes of all sizes and descriptions mothballed and folded away in attics. The meet is at eleven tomorrow and well within hacking distance."

I had done a fair amount of riding as a schoolboy and had hunted in a not very adventurous part of Southern England but my heart sank, as I looked at the field-borders of craggy walls and hairy banks, and at their frequency owing to the small size of the fields. Then I recalled that the last time I had ridden was with Lee over the Kowloon Hills and my spirit sank. My riding muscles, indeed all my muscles, were unfit and the anticipation of frightful stiffness acted as a counter-irritant to gloomy forebodings.

The next day dawned fair. The ancient, deciduous trees, close round the house, winter leafless, were like a regiment of goblins filtering the morning sun. Further back, dark conifers shut out all horizons. Caroline made up a glorious, full-belly breakfast. Fed and appreciative, I remarked, "In Ireland one should eat breakfast at every meal." She looked away and, with a strange bitterness, said, "At one time, in this country, the only food was potatoes, until the potato crops failed."

Sharp at ten, Seamus the doctor's groom clattered into the ill-kept yard. He was riding a big, rangy, chestnut horse, with a complicated bit in its mouth, and leading a small, grey mare, almost pony size. They were both trace clipped and looked thin but very fit.

The young groom was a small, dark, alert, Ibero-Celt. I could visualise him in a pub, animated but not obstreperous. "There y'are, Miss Caroline. Them is fit to jump the Bank of Ireland and the doctor says not to bring them home sweatin'."

He jumped off and handed us the reins. Turning to me with a welcoming smile, "Don't be deceived by the mare. She's little and small, but she'd clear the fence you would not see her ears behind it." I glanced nervously at the big, ribby horse and then found Seamus had one hand round my left ankle and I was flying up into the saddle. Seamus must have walked home.

It was about an hour's ride to the meet and, as we hacked along the deserted lanes, Caroline explained the horse to me.

"Don't worry about that contraption in his mouth. It's an invention of the doctor's, in case you get a slow hunt and he might get impatient and try to get his tongue over the bit; that horse knows his job and only has one idea in his little brain, to be up with hounds. Conditions are perfect for good scent and a fast run; there is bound to be a fox at Hangman's Cross." Caroline dropped the reins on the mare's neck and paused to light a cigarette and to let all this sink in. "All you have to do, Bob, is to sit there, don't mess around with his mouth and keep your weight forward off the horse's loin muscles. There will be very few people out, so you need not be afraid of a barging match but don't ride in the master's pocket."

Although my hunting jargon was rusty, I absorbed enough information to regain a little confidence, trying to remember the rhythm of swinging the upper part of my body forward a split second before the horse's forehand rose to the impending jump. As we arrived at the meet, a small, jolly crowd of riders and hangers-on were emerging from the pub at the crossroads; a few old men were holding the horses, discussing the whereabouts of a fox, which was accused of taking some woman's goose and goslings "and she a poor widow body." There was some friendly banter for me from a sprinkling of elderly Anglo-Irish remnants, a couple of vets, healthy-looking and confident, a priest, collared but otherwise in full hunting-turn-out, and some young men in rough clothes and wellington boots; one had reins and a bridle made of old rope. I paid little attention to all this; my nerves had tightened my throat and stomach muscles. There was a chorus of welcome for Caroline and we moved off to a nearby, gorse covert, not a quarter of a mile from the crossroads.

Hounds were put into the covert by the huntsman, a young semi-professional, who bore a striking resemblance to my host at Mountbriach and reminded me of Simon but with a peasant overlay.

The pack quickly got down to work with enthusiasm and there was little need for interference or encouragement from the hunt staff. Within a few minutes there arose heart-lifting hound music and it was apparent that they were on to a fox, which knew his ground and was unwilling to leave for the open.

Round and round they went, tow row row with plenty of scent in covert. I was enjoying a mixture of fearful anticipation and the excitement of the chase, when my blood ran cold with a different fear. The fox had become the submarine, turning and twisting below the cover of green water, the hounds a squadron of questing craft overhead. I must have paled visibly. Someone close by talked to his friend, *sotto voce*:

"Sure that one looks scared, them English fellows would hardly know which end of the horse is foremost."

My mind anticipated the crash of depth charges and, at that very moment, there was an eldritch, high-pitched call, for all the world like the scream of a treble descant. "Gone awaaoiy." A large, dark dog fox left the gorse running down-wind. The submarine would have turned the other way.

I shook the false image from my brain. There was a pause and then, at a nod from the master, a fine-looking, retired Colonel of the Irish Guards, the cavalry charge erupted. The small cavalcade fanned out and started to ride straight across the country in the wake of the flying pack. Caroline beside me said, "Look you could cover them with a pocket handkerchief." I settled down to let the horse do the work. "Samson" he was called and there was that sort of strength in his huge heave. I tried to steer without interfering with his mouth or loin muscles and to stay in the saddle. I forgot the submarine and remembered the old woman's slaughtered geese.

We tore across tiny fields, hardly recovering from a jump before the next one loomed.

The horse not only had a huge, natural spring but his jump was smooth and entirely within his control; my confidence increased but the run seemed endless and the spotted, pocket handkerchief, moving ahead of us, was gaining ground. I concentrated on keeping clear of and behind the master; the rest of the field had dropped behind. I saw the master's horse faltering, probably from a stone bruise and he waved me on. The huntsman ahead was alone, some way behind his pack. The whipper-in had been left at the wrong side of the gorse. I could not take in the country, just galloped and heaved over. There must have been a screaming scent and the going perfect, well-drained old pasture and firm. In an exhausted trance I felt that the hunt was for eternity. How could equine bone and muscle and wind stand up to it? Eventually the pace slowed. The huntsman was gaining on his pack; I was coming up with him, wondering if and how I could stop.

Suddenly it ended on a hillock in a small pile of rocks.

The huntsman jumped off his horse and flung the reins to me, calling off the hounds, which were sniffing round a crevice in the rocks, howling and whining, some pawing at the stones.

"The terriers will be no good here," he shouted above the din. "Sure it's like a quarry. The old man is not up with us but I will have to take them home now, no one will be able for anything after that and we must leave the fox on O'Sullivan's land. He will be ill-pleased and will want compensation; this fox will take an early lamb off him."

The field came up in ones and twos; the lad who had made a mock of me gave me an unabashed look of respect, so much so that I made some remark to transfer the glory to where it belonged, the sweating animal between my legs. We dismounted to rest the horses and slackened their girths awhile. Again I thought of the submarine safe behind its base defences.

Caroline said, "I can find a way back along the lane-ways; we will have to walk them all the way home to cool them and then bed them in the old loose-boxes."

As we walked towards home with the low sun at our backs, I ruefully anticipated the appalling stiffness which inevitably awaited me. I realised that, much as I needed to bed Caroline, for once I would not be able for it.

I got up next morning almost paralysed with stiffness and went off to say farewell and thank you to the old man. I found him pottering in an undusted gun room, musing over long unused guns and rods in racks on the walls. He turned to me, his eyes vacant, unrecognising. I thought that a quick shock might awake and unloose him. I could not have guessed how well I had hit the nail or what a dark secret had been concealed. After profuse thanks for his hospitality I said, as an aside, "By the way, sir, did you ever know Red O'Connor?"

The old man's eyes focused, not on me but on some distant figure not with us. "Colonel Rory Joyce O'Connor, of course, I knew him. He was our cousin. The Norman families mingled with the Irish in the way the newcomers seldom did. (I began to think that the relationship might be remote, the "newcomers" were Elizabethans!) "I was his Commanding Brigadier. A more gallant officer never stepped. I don't know how he did not get himself killed."

"But he did get killed," I broke in.

"No," the old voice was still firm, "he was not killed. In 1916, when the British shot the leaders of the Irish Rebellion, he was about to lead an attack. Colonels were not usually up in front – Red was. The day before the attack was due to go in, he came to me, his normally ruddy face white with emotion. I thought at first his nerve had cracked."

"Do you hear what they have done, Donald?" he said shaking with rage. "Shot them all in cold blood, Connolly, Pearse, the others, the whole west will be aflame. I cannot go on here; I intend to resign."

"You can't do that," I said, "they will shoot you. I would have to order it. This is what will be done. I have a Staff Colonel with battle experience who will take your place. I will announce in orders that you are to go on a special mission. You will simply disappear. Go to the back area with your rank and insignia and then black your hair and vanish. Do you want to go and fight for the rebels?"

"No," he said, "their cause is lost, for the time, and I have two loyalties." He sat with his head in his hands.

I patted his shoulder and said, "And get really lost, for the duration of the war, for if you are found, I will be shot. I am going to post you as missing, believed killed." I paused, "What about your little girl?"

"My cousin Roderick is looking after her. He is totally reliable. I see the wisdom of your judgement. I have no doubts about my ability to vanish." He stammered some thanks which I broke off with, 'Go now and God be with you.' I see all this as clearly as if it were yesterday." Then he suddenly lost his lucidity and seemed to think it was all a dream.

There was a long time to go before we could start our journey home. I assumed that Caroline would come with me. A pony trap would take me to the station. The train did not depart until noon and was slow and uncertain, running on peat as there was no coal. We decided to walk in the woods. Caroline then announced the shattering news that she was remaining to look after her uncle, who, she said, had not long to live. I did not feel justified in pleading with her to change her mind, but, perhaps, in a mood of lonely nostalgia, I asked if she had ever known Lee O'Connor. "I knew her in Hong Kong," I said. "She came from this part of the world, very bright, her mother was Chinese."

Caroline looked up sharply. "Lee is my cousin. Her mother was not Chinese, she was Japanese."

I was still feeling fairly soggy from too much port in my bloodstream, but this news shocked me into alertness. I had realised that Lee was Simon's cousin but "For the love of Mike, what was her story?"

"It is little known outside the family. It reads like an opera. The secret was well-kept, in a remote Irish village, on the west coast behind the mountains." Caroline was silent for a few minutes thinking of the past, perhaps wondering if she would tell me. "Lee's mother was the daughter of a Japanese naval officer; he came of one of the leading families of Japan, descended from the Shoguns. He became an admiral. Lee's mother was sent on a journey with suitable entourage to visit a relative in Singapore, travelling by steamer which called at Shanghai to take on passengers. Chinese pirates infiltrated the passengers and during the voyage, were able to overpower the crew and guards and force the ship to sail into Bias Bay, the port on the coast where pirates held sway. The girl was sold to a Chinese millionaire in Hong Kong. He was old and treated her with respect but kept her confined in his well-guarded palace. She did not commit suicide, as might have been expected of her, owing to her certainty that her father would rescue her. Her fate, however, lay elsewhere. Red O'Connor was an officer in one of the Irish regiments in the British Army; he was serving at the time in Hong Kong on the

Governor's staff. He was said to have been the best-looking man
ever; not merely handsome and static and pleased with himself as are
so many good-lookers. He was dashing, lively, good company and
humorous, an all-round sportsman and he had everything going for
him. He was invited to dinner by the Chinese millionaire and,
afterwards, one of the household was detailed to show him the
grounds and gardens. His guide led him past guards but must have
been improperly briefed for they walked into a group of women to
whom the guide chattered. O'Connor found himself with a strangely
beautiful girl, who spoke some English and was able to tell the story
of her incarceration in low tones. I suppose they fell in love with each
other's beauty at that moment.

Red O'Connor, having had a good look at the defences of the
palace and realising that the old man had somewhat let his guard
down, mounted a clandestine operation and kidnapped the girl.

All would have been well, had she, as would have been expected,
returned to her family in Japan. The scandal would have been hushed
up; but no, she was madly in love with Red and refused to leave him.
Red had to quit the Colony and the army and they went to live in his
cousin's family home on the west coast here, taking with them the
Chinese Amah who had attended her and was also included in the
kidnapping. After this terrific burst of initiative and transfer to a
foreign land, something must have weakened within her. She died
giving birth to Lee. They had never married. Red volunteered for the
1914 war; he was reported missing, believed killed."

My rather dull and inactive mind had, I think, been considerably
sharpened up by the exigencies of fighting and continuous campaign
on the enemy's doorstep. Immediately, pennies began to drop,
terrible possibilities began to occur to me. Lee had lied to me about
her mother. She had something to conceal. What was it? A Japanese
admiral in Hong Kong? Who was his very bright agent with an entrée
everywhere? What did Simon know of all this? Why had he drifted
away from my friendship? I was silent, struggling with my thoughts.
Caroline patted my arm. "Don't worry. Everyone fell in love with
Lee. No one could resist her nor hold her." I made no reply. The
train's departure was many hours late.

The engine, emitting purple smoke from the turf-fed boiler, took,
it seemed, forever to crawl out of the glorious, western mountain
ranges and across the dull, flat, central bog and back to the coastal rim

rising about Dublin City, its streets once again ringing to the clop of horse-drawn traffic for there was no petrol. I was not very observant of the journey. I realised that Caroline was leaving me.

Chapter Seventeen

Desperate Venture

Many months after my return from Ireland, with many depth charges in the debit of my endurance account, I climbed slowly up the gangway, which sloped up from the top of the submarine's bridge to the deck of a great battleship, the flagship at Scapa Flow. Tired and light-headed, I recalled Campbell's verse:

> "Britannia needs no bulwarks,
> No towers along the steep;
> Her march is o'er the mountain waves,
> Her home is on the deep."

Right now her march was in Scapa Flow. On deck I saluted mechanically at the shrill skirl of boatswain's pipes. Then my heart lifted. I looked into the beaming welcoming face of Bumble Harp, my flotilla mate of early days on the China Coast. Talking to Bumble was like shooting into a blanket, your shafts didn't wound, your shots could not ricochet. I was glad to see Bumble safely ensconced in the flagship. I thought he wouldn't fit in the awful discomfort of a war-time submarine; thought he wouldn't be tough enough to take it near the enemy. How wrong I proved to be. Bumble, later an audacious submarine captain, charged an enemy harbour and, while caught in the nets, managed to torpedo an enemy troopship at anchor, before the local defences blew him up; now all he wanted to do was to minister to my comfort. "Bob, hero, come down for a bath, the C-in-C is away and the staff are busy but you're to dine in the cuddy; you know the Flags from China days, Simon Dunbulben he was, just become Mountbriach and inherited a bog somewhere in Ireland. You and he and I and your Number One. I think Simon has been told to pump you about your last patrol, the admiral's steward is breaking out the No. 1 port, only used for VIPs."

So the old man had left his musty sanctum; the old house would tumble in. Who would care for the ageing retainers? I shivered. Caroline had told me about the harsh county home. We chatted amiably, moving down to my cabin and then to the luxury of the bathroom, where we tubbed and showered and I cleaned off three weeks of dirt. You can't get dirtier than dirty, after a bit it drops off.

Bumble said, "I wouldn't know you, Bob, as the Champion Gymnast of your year, those muscles need a tone-up."

"Yes," I said, looking down sadly, "they are quite useless in this life trying to use up the minimum of oxygen. I should have been a commando; unused muscle seems to be an adversity."

We assembled at the admiral's table for dinner. Simon on my left, cheerful and ironic. I thought he'd probably heard that I'd been seen around with Caroline, but I didn't want to enlighten him and we talked about our China Coast incarnation, a sort of 'iridescence of decay' banter.

The dinner, fresh food and good service seemed like a feast of the gods. After the table was cleared and the stewards had withdrawn, we were left with the port, all young enough to talk without inhibition. Tom was encouraged to hold the table. His keen brain was recognised and he had a friend connected with a pre-war, military mission to Russia, which gave him a window on the world.

"What about holding the ring now, Tom," I said, "it's bulging a bit."

Tom said, "We've held some sort of a ring for all my lifetime with bluff. The huge battlefleet, that sat in Malta all our youth was obsolete at Jutland. The German Commander-in-Chief said, "Build me an unsinkable gun platform" and he got it, an armoured honeycomb. Ours were glorified yachts for Edwardian gentry. My history professor told me we couldn't build the honeycomb type because they had to operate all over the world and would be too uncomfortable. Well, they sat in a Maginot line in Scotland; these new ones are no better. The RAF and RN pulled the maritime airforces into two inadequate parts; we've no fast tankers or support ships to keep the fleet at sea, even Nelson had victuallers. My destroyer pal tells me he fought stukas with not one gun elevating above fourteen degrees. He said he saw a gunlayer throw an empty beer bottle at them."

Simon broke in, "Yes, Tom, and I can vouch that your stuff isn't hindsight. I remember you spouting all this at the War course. Everyone thought you were crazy and especially the bit in your paper after reading the Russo Jap War of 1904, something about 'as the Jap soldiers threw themselves on the Russian bayonets', the Jap fighters would charge the ship's bridges. Well, the Japs won't interfere. They wouldn't want a Russian threat.

Tom resumed, "I had dinner with my Russian link not long ago; he told me, in measured terms and without cover of secrecy, not to worry about an imbalance of manpower. Frankly, I don't believe him; also I don't know that I admire Stalin for killing the kulaks any more than Hitler for hanging the Jews, but it would be a sort of comfort to have five million greycoats with their bayonets pointed at someone else."

After a bit more in this vein, we loosened up and the port started to work. Simon said, "The staff will be pulling your report to pieces soon, Bob. The admiral wants to know the secrets of your great heart and tiny brain on the direct line."

I don't know what I told them through an increasing haze, of which the loosening effect seemed to run a losing race with oblivion. So here is what I can remember now.

We had been stuck right in off the coast of Norway. It was mid-summer; there was no darkness. After about twenty hours underwater, the battery power was in need of recharge, which meant we must get to the surface to reach for air to work the diesel engines and generators. Worse, we began to breathe like asthmatics, the oxygen was running very low. "Lucky we can't smoke," said the Chief, who struck a match which would not light. Another unseen foe was reaching for us; the carbon dioxide content of the air was rising towards a highly poisonous state; the leaks from the high pressure air system were building up a pressure that increased the power of our toxic enemies. I had got to know the routines of the methodical German air patrols. I made a dash for the surface immediately after one had disappeared; like going out-of-doors just as a shower is stopping, you have fine weather till the next. I knew it could not last; someone would come out of phase. Hunter killer groups of anti-submarine vessels were around. The home radio was incessantly calling other submarines in our vicinity which should now have been home. Suddenly, it came to me or was it Tom thought of it? I think it was. He said, "The crew can't take much more, sir, or I'll have good men making blathering idiot mistakes." The weather was calm. We slowly crept in under the Norwegian cliffs; no one would suspect us there. The airmen wouldn't see us close under the land, and, if we were surprised, the bombing attack could not be pressed home.

We surfaced close to the rocks. It reminded me of circling Portland Bill in a dinghy inside the tide race: you touch the rocks with one hand, the tide race boils a few yards out. The towering cliffs were like an umbrella. So we stayed and pumped in air. I realised we were in a useless position. The enemy ships kept further out. I also realised that, if we made an attack and fixed ourselves, we were doomed. After the initial surprise and fear at an exposure on the surface wore off, a sort of relieved jollity spread through us; somebody made the joke about Piccadilly Underground again and someone even sang the bawdy little jingle. I was wondering if I ought to be shot for cowardice, when up the hatch on to the bridge shot a messenger with a signal. "Damaged enemy cruiser may seek refuge in Wolfheim Fjord." Just that, it left action to me.

The fjord was a long, narrow gash in the high rocky coast, too steep for even a fishing village, no fixed defences, a good lair for a wounded wolf. Every commanding officer must have the burning desire to get at the enemy – did I tell Simon that I'd lost that burn? The fjord was forty miles south of us. I'd take two days to get there, with a rock-side charge-up on the way, and arrive with a fairly full battery and only half-exhausted air supply. I'd go in at dawn, God help me, would I? The grapevine telegraph soon spread the news but the crew were past generating a new tension.

(Only after the war were the physiological and psychological effects of prolonged oxygen lack and carbon dioxide poisoning fully understood. It was better not to understand what you couldn't help.)

I could no longer see the people around me, only visualise the narrow hole in the cliff, the lurking defenders. Frank Girling's gypsy tan had not altered during these months of underwater groping. The hybrid vigour of a more primitive race seemed indestructible. I knew he could go on applying his built-in skill, without the lessening energy, which everyone else seemed to be feeling. We went carefully over the tidal streams and currents and took innumerable fixes off the coast to check up for the last run in; the actual entrance was described as "hidden by a curtain of rock". We would have to make the entry underwater. The place was too narrow to turn while we dived; we would have either to come out astern or surface and then turn. We must sink the opposition but no aircraft could attack us in the cleft. There was a little bay-form at the head of the fjord, where ships could lie, too deep to anchor but, with boats, they could get lines out to the rocks. We crept towards what seemed an unbroken line of cliffs, in a midsummer half-night; Frank's ceaseless work was now aided by the enemy. There it was, two trawlers patrolling to and fro across the entrance. I'd got to know the ways of these; I could calculate their sentry go and find the moment to glide in at their turn and they helped my straining eyes to see the hole. Some fool dropped a spanner, "clink". I could see a question-mark on the nearest trawler's face. She must have thought it was her own noise and went on with her leisurely vigil. We slid down between the cliffs; now it was easy, like the peacetime exercises we did round the cliffs in Malta.

We had six torpedoes, no chance of a reload, the chaps outside would see to that; we must sink them all with one go; all, because I knew the cruiser must have dogs-of-war with her. What was I going to do with my torpedoes? Was a submarine expendable against a cruiser? The diving hydroplanes whirred to and fro, but I could no longer see the friendly backs of Max Pell and Martin Smith. Tom breathed his orders like a smuggler, my periscope rose, spun and lowered; the trawlers quickly disappeared behind us. The cliff face on either side looked close enough in normal vision and when I put the periscope to high power magnification I could see insects on the rock. At last we burst into the bay. There she lay, the cruiser, badly listing, roped somehow to the rocks and probably unable to work her guns, with two destroyers, one on either side lightly attached, ready.

I swung slowly across them all and fired as the sights came on. This is what happened. Two torpedoes hit and sank the first destroyer, the next shot at the cruiser ran crooked and blew up on the rocks, the fourth shot hit the cruiser's side, clonk, and did not explode, the fifth and sixth both hit the second destroyer and up she blew.

I had no time for regrets then. I knew we would never make it out astern and those bastards outside would be in, pell-mell, soon, but not too quickly as they would not want to foul up the destroyers, until they realised they were fouled up already.

As the boat sprung to the surface, I let go the upper hatch with trembling fingers and clung on while the air pressure, vented from the torpedo tubes, whooshed past me. Tom had the periscope up and was already giving the motor orders ahead and astern to turn us round. As I took over, I could see men on the cruiser rushing to some light automatics. They were a bit slow and we were nearly end-on by the time their shots pattered round us, chipping bits off the casing, bouncing off the tough pressure hull. I had one man with me. He gave a cry and leant forward. I saw his chest was blown away and had to heave his dead body clear of the motor order telegraphs. We dived again as the patter of shots became a roar. The dead body must have swirled off to its lonely funeral.

The fjord was tortuous but we could keep at periscope depth until these trawlers came in. The cruiser would signal them; we'd have time to get pointed for the entrance. The men were elated by the crash of torpedo hits. Bill Frazer looked in smiling and said:

"The fore-end men are polishing up the warhead safety pins for mementoes."

Harshly, I croaked, "Get back forward and prepare for depth charging."

Yes, here they were, charging up the fjord towards us, behind them a peep of open water. Down we bounced under them. They let off patterns by guesswork, not close but, owing to the narrow rock fjord, it was like letting off bombs in a whispering gallery. The noise and reverberations deafened and dazed everyone; errors in operation quickly started and a firm grip of supervision had to be imposed. One didn't want to be killed by a loud bang. I'd never heard the like of it. Patterns, which we had previously experienced straddling us, seemed like pop guns in comparison. Tom wiped his brow and said, "If that was a distant one, what's it like close to?"

We now made out into the open sea, the never darkening sky above. Our trawlers weren't much good, but good enough to hang on and call up their friends. Down in the depths we could hear them chug around and drop their beastly messages of destruction. After many hours, the crew around me panted like dogs in the foul atmosphere. I'd now time to sum it up. I should have sunk the cruiser and taken my medicine from the destroyers. I'd saved our lives in the bay by a coward's act – now we were going to lose them by long, slow suffocation. I didn't like the situation, perhaps one thing was a counter-balance to the other.

We should have gone down, both as a punishment from the gods and by the hopelessness of our situation.

Two things saved us: Tom found a layer of dense water on which the submarine could sit and save battery power and whatever gods there were sent a little summer storm above us. Disturbed water, wind, rain, darkness, escape.

I couldn't look at my crew for a bit. Chief's indirect asides showed me that they didn't blame me. They were delighted to escape with their lives, but pleased to add the score of two destroyers but sad, of course, at the death of a shipmate.

Simon looked quizzical throughout the tale. All he wanted was to get a clear picture for his master, particularly of how bad the cruiser was.

Suddenly, I realised that I was going to do something I hadn't done since childhood. I wanted to weep. I thought that I should not let Simon see or he would tell the old man my nerve had cracked. I feigned drunkenness and lurched off to my cabin. I had the sense to put a towel on the pillow.

Chapter Eighteen

Running Down

Next morning I said to Simon, "I must get to London quick to see Admiral Submarines. I'd like to leave the boat here. Please get the spare crew captain flown up to drive her back to base and please fly me down."

Simon said, "Oh yes, I'm sure you must see your Admiral. I'll ask the staff to oblige. You won't lose any time." He looked away, betraying the fact that he knew about my real motive. I'd heard that Caroline was back in London. I forbore to question Simon about his cold attitude; there were two possible explanations. I felt that he must know and disapprove of my relationship with Caroline, which appeared to be ending. Possibly he was attracted to her, as I suspect that he had been to Lee. Caroline had unlimited sex appeal. Or, and perhaps also, he disapproved of her knock-about lifestyle. I pondered for a while, thinking "it will pass." As my plane drew south it became apparent that there were heavy air raids and we did a few diversions. Simon's magic passwords got me a staff car into London. I made an excuse and told the pretty Wren driver to drop me at the back of the mews. The shambles around me showed that a stick of bombs had fallen down the street. "Christ," I said half-aloud, "like a pattern of depth charges." My heart was in my mouth as I picked my way across a glacier of broken windowpanes. There had been a hit in the mews opposite Caroline's flat, a chunk of masonry or something had ploughed through her roof but otherwise the building stood. Caroline sat on the steps outside, smoking a cigarette. Her face was streaked with dust, her hair hung lank and her eyes were bleak. She looked shocked, spiritually pulverised.

There was no welcome in her glance. She didn't get up. "Don't go in, Bob. There is a dead man in my room. I was in the kitchen."

"Is it a Frenchman?" I said, unnecessarily. Then I hoped she'd come to me, cry or something.

She didn't but said levelly, "In the books about free love, it's always all right, no one has a baby, no one has VD – those things aren't right any more. Please go away, Bob. The man inside needs the ARP burial squad and I've rung them; I need a whore's doctor – I've rung him."

I picked up a girl in Piccadilly Circus, large, her hair dyed red, stupid, friendly and nice. We went to her flat and sometime later she got up and brewed some tea. "Cripes," she grumbled, "what's wrong with you? Sex maniac or something, like making love to a ruddy thunderstorm. Reckons you owes me double." She chatted, good-heartedly, while we drank the tea.

I spent the night in the dark, Victorian interior of a service club for officers and gentlemen. I felt sorry about Caroline. I'd always pictured myself as an unselfish, giving sort of person. Now I'd fallen down a well and I felt more sorry for myself than for her. I didn't know what the hell I was going to do without her.

Next day I shrank up to Submarine Headquarters. After the washup I didn't get shot or even sacked. Mostly, I think, because we were short of replacements. I was given a mild wigging and a second bar to my DSC but I could see the authorities thought I should have a posthumous VC and the cruiser. So did I. Three aircraft were shot down subsequently allacking the thing and she finally got home to Germany. The two destroyers were rather small ones, perhaps frigates.

I took the train back to Edinburgh to join the boat at our new base. Tom met me at the station with a naval car. "There's a bit of a do on tomorrow night," he said. "The ship's Company have organised some dance hall. They'd like us along."

"Oh, lord," I said, "that means too much drink and don't pinch the sailor's girls. That gypsy navigator is too good-looking, better keep him aboard as duty officer."

I postponed working on the patrol report, I'd done enough of that by mouth,and caught up on some gigantic sleep deficits and also with the latest drink fashion, rum and milk. Why it had superseded temporarily the usual gin routine I can dimly guess. I spruced up a bit for the dance, we all piled into a private bus and I began to thaw out towards the men, who rapidly became jolly and incoherent. I still had a more than usual shocked strain in me, which had the effect of keeping me abnormally sober; pretty soon I realised my sobriety was dividing me from the rest, a haze of flushed faces become too companionable to pay enough attention to the women. I then made my big error and started to eye up Lisa. She wasn't having much fun and we had two or three dances. I'd no idea who she was nor did I ask; she wore no wedding ring but there was a groove on the third finger of her let hand. She was dark with the square beauty of the lowland Scot, rather blurred by town living, young and firm-breasted. I whispered a plan and we soon escaped unnoticed. She said that she had borrowed a flat and, to my surprise, we came in through a musty, middle-class house to a room of surprising luxury and bizarre furnishings. A huge four-poster bed in one corner was half curtained with red, velvet hangings. The wallpaper, faded green with cornucopia patterns, must have been a hundred years old. I'd no idea where we were nor in whose house.

About two hours later, Lisa slept, snoring a little in the crook of my shoulder. I was still awake and contemplating rousing her, when a crashing sounded through the house, the door opened and in tottered Max Pell and Martin Smith, arm-in-arm, rocking drunk and behind them a Petty Officer from some other ship with a woman. I feigned sleep with half-opened lids, thank God Lisa did not wake. Martin Smith started forward with a terrible oath; Lisa must have been his date at some time. Pell's huge fist shot out and dropped him in his tracks. Presently, after a lot of whispering, the strange couple disappeared next door and our pair went to sleep in chairs. When they were well asleep, I woke Lisa by pinching her nose gently. She didn't see the others, until it was too late to change her mind, and then I muffled her exclamations with my palm.

In the morning, I thought there would be a scene, which would end in court martial, but everyone behaved as if nothing unusual had occurred; someone brewed tea and served it with a tot of whisky in each cup. I piled into a taxi with the Petty Officers and we drove through the lovely morning, arriving back on board our ship by the regulation time, 7.30. No one ever mentioned the incident again.

Frazer came into my cabin as I was shaving. "There's a panic on, sir. Some sort of invasion scare. We've to go to short notice for sea. I've started loading fish now, all the latest torpedoes, mark eights;

they're supposed to work and go off. They've used up the 1914 war stock now. Number One says he's recalled Chief from leave."

"Poor little bugger," I said. I could well realise the agony of parting from the love of one's heart. How could it be stood at all? Or did the strength of their union give an added spiritual fortitude? I looked at myself in the mirror, tired and debauched. I tried to match the past and future. There was no chance of losing my nerve now. I'd lost it some time ago; not suddenly in a breakdown, but slowly, in little drops of sweated-out surplus carbon dioxide, in a million pants for vanishing oxygen, in an eternity of fear and forethought. I was a sort of zombie undead: not much use to my side. I'd lost the fire but perhaps there was something left. The blind king of Bohemia was carried into battle by his knights; I would put out my arms and let my sound crew carry me. In a fervour of thought train, I put out my arms but instead of a sword, I carried a safety razor, which cracked sharply against the steel bulkhead.

The signalman knocked and pulled back the cabin curtain. "Signal from "S" (six), sir, come to immediate notice for sea." Private, from C-in-C's Flag Lieutenant, "Congratulations on your decoration," and a telegram, "Regret suffering jaundice, duration sickness unknown, Signed Lamb." "First Lieutenant has recalled the non-duty watch off leave, sir." He bobbed out as I grunted. Tom looked in before I'd finished reaping.

"This is a bit of a bind, sir. We are scraping the bottom of the barrel for engineers. There is someone in the spare crew, a sub-lieutenant. The only report my spies give me is that he was a stoker, but he went sick so they made him an officer: sort of garbled but I don't think he will do."

The fact that Tom, my closest friend, consistently addressed me by the respectful vocative, 'sir' added a touch of unreality to dramatic situations; furthermore I was always reluctant to override him. However, I had paid a recent visit to the Submarine Base Drafting Officer.

I replied, "We can't pull someone out of the bag from the base. The Chief Engine Room Artificer will have to carry the weight and the local lad will be a figurehead."

I washed the suds off my face. "Our Chief ERA is the best submarine engineer in the western hemisphere. The only reason he is not an officer is because he won't do book-learning and exams. The stoker Petty Officer could keep discipline with a crew of mutinous wild cats; we'll take that young lad and after four patrols he will be an officer – or a nutcase."

Tom grasped the facts at once and, after a pause for thought, replied "Yes, and the Officers' Mess will need to give him all the support which he needs."

Tom went out and I thought a bit more. "This process is going to continue. Most of the old hands have been sunk. We are building new submarines as fast as we can. If we gradually accumulate a crew of greenhorns, I will have to be an officer, in leadership and technology, not an old blind king. It's a bit late now. I'll have to pull my socks up, perhaps pull myself out of other people's beds." I let that train of thought peter out and ambled off to stoke up with a huge breakfast, for which those sort of evenings gave me an unhealthy appetite.

This, then, was our life, chase, find, escape: but the chase was always after us. Our side was being knocked down like nine-pins in an alley. The summer of 1940 rolled into autumn and the merciful darkness started to give us an air-raid shelter by night. The look out's sharpness was a guarantee that no ship, which threw a bow wave or a glow from its funnels, would get into sparring distance, unseen in the dark. The worst enemy was the low moon which threw a silhouette: always point stern toward her so that you were fleeing from the danger quarter, where a man had you in his sights, into the paler light of safety.

I was called down to Submarine Headquarters in London. I'd not heard from Caroline and this time went straight to my duty – well almost, I couldn't help walking past the mews. I was interviewed by a junior staff officer who concealed his distaste for his desk work by forced joviality.

"Well, Bob, you've set us a problem by surviving; your boat is overdue for its eighteen-monthly refit. There isn't a home dockyard free to take you on: lots of head scratching. Don't shoot me; you are to go out to Singapore." My heart rose and fell in waves. I wouldn't have to be chased around by a relentless enemy – I thought. My crew would go to pieces in the Far East. My boat would not get a proper refit in inexperienced hands. Well, at least, I wouldn't go to pieces. I was in pieces already.

The immediate problem was that I would have to take the boat out through a hostile Mediterranean, probably doing operations on the way, and she was at her last gasp, poor, old girl. I made some idiotic joke about Singapore more far and he said, "I'm afraid the drafting people will strip down your crew a bit. They need the old stagers for the new construction submarines. You will have time to shake down the new boys."

The eastward journey spun out into a lengthy Odyssey. At each port of call, the battered submarine threatened to lumber to a halt. The wardroom was filled with new faces. The Chief Engineer, Sub-lieutenant Shavin, had slowly built himself into a competent officer on the backs of the old sweats who were now mostly disappearing. Tom, of course, went, to qualify for Commanding Officer, Bill Frazer became first lieutenant, and Frank Girling had been replaced by "Spike" Spurgeon, straight from his training class and looking like a scrubbed schoolboy. He had very small navigational skill, but the way to the shiny East is easier to follow than the riddles of the storm-lashed sands of the North Sea.

It was easy to knock the new element of the crew into some sort of shape, during the twelve hundred mile journey from Gosport to Gibraltar. At Gib we had engine trouble and a long spell in the dockyard.

The monotonous, onward voyage towards Singapore, when compared to our previous action-packed operations, seemed likely to continue for eternity. The submarine needed not so much a refit as a rebuild. We staggered from one outpost of Empire to another, each one proud and remote, with the silhouette of a crouching lion. The lion had crouched for a long time now, surrounded, embattled, not daring to spring. Gibraltar, Malta, Port Said, no, the latter did not look like a crouching lion, Aden and Ceylon, yes they did. In the ports, in which we rested, swarms of dockyard people tacked up our hull and machinery. After each dockyard patch-up, the operational staff could not forebear to send us on a war patrol, so desperate was then the need to cut the enemies' communication with North Africa. These patrols resulted in humiliating failure, with the breakdown of vital machinery and the doubtfulness of our ability to struggle back to base; things like having no high pressure air to blow out the ballast tanks to regain the surface. I wondered if it was the boat breaking – or me.

In Malta, we endured some very sharp bombing attacks, accurate and determined, which narrowly missed putting an end to the voyage. One of the other commanding officers complained that an enemy fighter had machine-gunned him through the window of his bedroom, as he drank his early morning tea.

I had drawn an enormous strength here from contact with the flotilla, which was in sharp contrast to our earlier efforts off Norway: there our huge casualty rate, about seventy-five per cent, had resulted in little damage to the enemy behind their defences. In the Mediterranean, great efforts were made to reinforce and supply the German armies in North Africa and, though again with frightful casualties, my comrades had torn great pieces out of the stream of shipping, which had to cross the breadth of the landlocked sea. I enjoyed renewing old friendships but, at the same time, began to slip into a remote, reclusive, loveless world; with little regret I bid farewell to the great honey-coloured fortress of Valetta and there followed an uneventful passage through the Eastern Mediterranean to Port Said.

I learned with mixed feeling that Tom had been diagnosed tuberculous, that he had been removed from submarine service and suitably drafted into Naval Intelligence for special service. He would, I supposed, now never rise to the high rank, which would have been his due and would probably contract a humble marriage; at least he would live.

Chapter Nineteen

Split Loyalties

Linking the embattled Mediterranean to the Indian Ocean, the Suez Canal had now become the main artery of the British Empire. In order to operate as a blood cell moving in the general circulation, my submarine required another refit.

The Canal Company operated an excellent dockyard at Port Said and here we repaired for a while. The opulence of the establishment was emphasised by the workmen's pissoir which was made of blue marble; so might Pharaoh have urinated.

I was housed at a comfortable hotel near the waterfront; a luxurious interlude, which was interrupted by a visitor in civilian clothes, with an identification from Special Operations Executive and written instructions to act under his orders. We sat on the verandah of my room, the sun low on my left hand, a long gin drink to the right: beer would have attracted a swarm of flies on the marble-topped table. My visitor was secretive and did not divulge his name, only exhibiting the cards of officialdom.

I was stirred by unease stemming from two memories. One was of a chance conversation with Simon about clandestine operations. In one response to some of my doubts, he had said, "Private armies are being infiltrated by Communists." I also recalled that one of my friends had been refitting his submarine in a shipyard, where the workforce went on a strike, which had been fomented by communists. Stalin was at this time a back-up ally for Hitler.

I could not control the command chain, but I had a sharp instinct for watching my own back. My new controller was friendly and well-mannered. He had abundant, light brown hair and those bushy eyebrows which exude authority. After some initial, polite chat, he led off:

"We are sorry to make this last-minute demand on you. The Commander-in-Chief has authorised the use of your submarine to land a very important agent in Italy. The decision to use your battered vessel was based on the fact of your considerable personal experience and apparent survival factor."

I took a pull at my drink – no man is immune to flattery. My visitor continued, "The success of the drop is of such importance that you must on no account betray your position by attacking enemy vessels, no matter how tempting may be the target. Written orders will follow."

He passed me a slip on which was printed the latitude and longitude of the beach where we should land our man by folbot. I could see at a glance that the beach was somewhere deep into the Adriatic. The conduct of the operation was to be largely left to me, the timing geared to the dark of the moon. Little remained to be discussed: we drank up and parted affably.

Alone on the balcony I considered the situation which caused me foreboding. I had little confidence in the functional capacity of my submarine and scepticism at being out of the normal chain of command. The thought of holding fire from a major target was utterly repugnant. I later made an effort to get permission to fire, if a U-boat presented itself, (the U-boats were at that time winning the war for Germany and constituted prime targets). The answer was, "No". I wonder if our agent intended to assassinate Hitler and win the war single-handedly.

He came on board shortly before we sailed, a slim man of medium height with Italianate good looks. I realised at once that I had seen him before, but could not recall the occasion. I thought to myself, 'It will come back to me.' He carried a rustic haversack, from which he abstracted his toilet gear, and then asked me to lock the rucksack in the chest of drawers for confidential books.

We sat alone in the wardroom, sweltering in the heat, given off by the steel hull exposed to the midday sun. I had told my second-in-command to pilot the boat out of harbour to sea, in order to give him the confidence he would soon need, when he came to take over his first command.

"My name is Luigi," said our visitor, with no trace of a foreign accent. He continued, "I speak perfect regional Italian. All you have to do is to put me ashore." I had brought on board a strong Royal Marine Sergeant and a two-man folding canoe for this purpose.

Silence fell between us. There was a muted, undulant throbbing from the electric main motors now being used to manoeuvre the boat out of harbour.

I think it was Luigi's next crass remark which started to jog my memory. "Are you not anxious, sitting down here helpless, while that young man is piloting you out to sea?" Driven by my abnormal mood, I made a dismissive rejoinder, "Anxiety is relative."

The wardroom light was dim compared with the harsh Egyptian sun. I knew that I had seen Luigi before. It was at Hong Kong, in the Yacht Club. I had been talking to Lee; we had been for a short sail in someone's day racer. Luigi was in close conversation with Simon: they were sitting at a table some distance from us. Luigi had turned and Lee had given a slight hand wave of recognition to which he responded. I assumed that he, slim and beautiful, was Simon's boyfriend. We did not join them and left separately.

My mind returned to the present. We exchanged some gossip. I wanted to calm the atmosphere. Then I cut in, without preamble,

"Surely I have seen you before. I think it was at the Royal Hong Kong Yacht Club, sometime in the early thirties?" Luigi was taken well off balance and, for an instant, he wore a hunted expression. He was saved from further interrogation by the fact that I had a different, far greater interest than his identity. Without waiting for his reply, I asked, "Have you any idea what happened to Lee O'Connor?"

I had lost one advantage, but I had another far greater need to know. At that moment, the electric motors fell silent, spinning idly on their shafts, ready to act as dynamos, to charge the main batteries which I knew to be nearing their life's end, like an old pet dog who can hardly rise up on his hind legs. The diesel engines were being clutched in and, after a few initial coughs, there was a satisfying roar, and we were on our way.

I was still looking enquiringly at Luigi, willing him to speak. "Yes, I well remember Lee in Hong Kong. She was a first-class sailor. I was a lecturer at the University and part owner of a small cruising yacht. One loses track of people in the fog of war. I seem to remember that Lee was connected with some important project in the USA."

He was tapping his knee and it occurred to me that he was not such a good secret agent as might have been assumed from our orders and that he was being evasive and probably lying. I forbore to ask him about Simon, the trail was too muddy.

We made a particularly cautious passage towards and into the Adriatic, diving by day and even by night, when there was a low full moon, avoiding focal points for shipping and going deep below the surface on still, clear days to avoid detection by aircraft and, by night, turning away or diving at the hint of another vessel.

It was irritating for us all to be playing the ultimate coward. My own irritation was increased by the feeling, more intuitive than rational, that Luigi had the ability to divulge information about Lee, information which he could not give without compromising himself. I forced my mind from its hopeless yearning towards the unfolding problem which confronted me.

The German National Socialists and the United Soviet Socialist Republic were still in league. I had been given warning of Communist infiltration, even into our Command structure. "Reds under the beds" was no longer a joke. I also knew that, on some occasions, submarines involved in clandestine operations had had their positions compromised, probably by agents who had been turned or who were double agents in origin.

I returned to an easy-going relationship with Luigi for a few days to let the dust settle. During this time, I made a habit of sitting up alone with him at night, when the other deck officers were on watch or asleep and the engineer officer was prowling around the shaky machinery. Luigi slept mostly by day. We had just finished drinking our mugs of tea over a discussion about sailing yachts around the South China Sea and I said, "Why don't you go up on the bridge for a breath of fresh air? Just ask permission from the Officer of the Watch through the voicepipe." The discussion about sailing had, as I hoped, put him in the mood for the feel of the wind on his face, and up he went.

Having previously obtained the key of the confidential chest, which was stowed in my cabin, I unlocked and drew out Luigi's sack. I knew that the Officer of the Watch was a gossip and would keep Luigi in conversation; he could not, of course, chat to the lookouts and distract their concentration. Also, I knew that I would be warned if Luigi came down the hatch untowardly early by the instant drop in air pressure on the eardrums, caused by his body obstructing the rush of air down the conning tower feeding the diesel engines.

I rummaged through Luigi's possessions. There was the usual unremarkable jumble of personal effects, which a peasant might take on a journey, and also some identity papers and letters. I guessed that, if he had anything to conceal, it was most likely designed to stand up to a cursory, unsophisticated examination. One stiff, thickish card had some verses printed in Italian, with a surround which indicated that they were religious. The back of the card was blank and the feel of it reminded me of some equipment which I had been shown in the Intelligence Centre at Malta. The handler had explained, "This will not stand up to sophisticated examination." I picked up my chart magnifying glass, put the card face down near a hundred watt electric light bulb and then, finding the focal length, I directed a heat stream through the magnifier on to the card. The two thin strips of which it was composed could then be slid apart to reveal on their inside borders of adhesive framing, two maps of Yugoslavia, one political, showing the centres of population, roads and ethnic grouping, the other physical. I traced with my fingers the spines of the great mountain ranges, some of which I had climbed during the era of the fading Pax Britannica. I reassembled the card with care and pressed it beneath a book, cooling it under a ventilation fan, and put everything back as it was, relocking the chest.

I had plenty of time to ruminate, sitting alone in the wardroom, having got the control room messenger to bring me another mug of hot, sweet tea.

It was late in March 1941. Russia was currently in a back-up alliance with Hitler. Prince Paul, Regent of Yugoslavia, had signed a pact with the axis. I could not have guessed how soon all this was to undergo a dramatic volte-face.

Luigi, for all his vaunted importance, appeared to be an agent of low calibre. I recalled again Simon's warning of communist infiltration into influential positions, creating a dangerous situation.

I had a sudden recall of memory. An incident at a hectic party in the Gloucester Buildings on Hong Kong, remote in time and always thrust into the back of my mind, now sprang into a clear vision of memory. Lee, surrounded by middle-aged men, worldly-wise and socially apt. Suddenly, a young, handsome man was talking earnestly to Lee. She hung on his words for a few moments before he faded into sudden invisibility; it was Luigi again, his etherial beauty standing out among the flushed middle-aged drinkers.

Commonsense dictated that, if he was bound for Yugoslavia he should have been landed there. I could not assemble the information which I held into a lucid consequence but I formed an increased determination to ensure that this operation should not backfire on us.

Chapter Twenty

Betrayed

The day following my discovery of Luigi's maps, I assembled the printed information concerning the droppings of our agent, the large scale chart of the northern Adriatic, a description of the environment in the Admiralty Sailing Directions, my secret orders and some photographs of the designated landing beach, taken through the periscope of one of our submarines. These photographs were not too clear and taken from long range. A sandy shelf jutted out from the beach so that, for about half a mile to seaward, there was insufficient depth of water to cover a submerged submarine. The beach inclined gently up towards the hinterland, which had poor soil, and was reedy and interspersed with marshes. The area was sparsely populated, defence and coast watching negligible or lapsed. There were no buildings in sight except the ruin of a fortified, small medieval manor at the north end of the beach. Halfway along the beach, stretching southward, there was a rocky bluff, about a hundred feet high, on the end of a small promontory. We were to surface when darkness fell, just outside the shallows and send Luigi straight in by canoe – simple.

I intended to execute a different plan. I would come in at nightfall, as ordered, but on the surface, silently, using the electric motors, right into the shallows but on a course which would keep the rocky bluff in line with the ruined manor. We would be horrifyingly close to the shore. I gave a shiver, recalling that passage of the Norwegian fjord in 1940. There was an adjacent enemy mine barrier, which our intelligence had pinpointed, and this was easy to skirt.

There were a few minor incidents, during the passage of the Adriatic and the approach to the area, mostly with fishing boats. They served to sharpen up the crew without posing any real danger. There were some good Italian anti-submarine operators but, in my experience, neither they, nor even the Japanese, when later I came up against them, measured up to the ferocity of some of the earlier German attacks.

We came towards our objective without harassment. A day was spent submerged to seaward of the beach and close in towards the shelf, while I prospected the bluff and the little ruined fort. There was no movement ashore, at sea or in the air, this area seemed to have stepped out of the war. I would have liked to have landed the canoe to the south of the bluff, but the terrain inland was too broken and waterlogged for a human crossing. It had to be the northern part of the beach.

So we would surface out of sight of the fort, creep up close under and to southward of the bluff, disembark the canoe, as quickly and silently as possible, (this action had been well rehearsed in harbour). Sergeant MacRae would paddle silently northward round the bluff to the beach, disembark Luigi and return, unobtrusive in the starlight, back round the bluff to re-embark in the submarine, where all would be anxiously awaiting his reappearance.

And thus it started to happen. There were no hitches, no noise, all machinery was switched off. Against the background noise of the cicadas, the initial violinists, sawing away with their hind legs, I could hear the tick of the stopwatch with which I was measuring the expected span of the journey. Fifteen seconds before his return was anticipated, MacRae came into sight round the bluff, precisely as a machine gun opened up an inaccurate fire at long range from the fort, the bullets kicking up splashes in a wide spread round the canoe now paddling furiously round the bluff, racing for shelter behind it to return to our welcoming arms. Now super-alert, I swept the seaward horizon with recently cleaned binoculars designed to enhance night vision. The first thing which you are likely to see of a fast-moving, small warship at night is the bow wave. A white feather was creaming down from northward, appearing abruptly from behind the seaward edge of the bluff. An enemy destroyer was racing towards the position about half to one mile off the beach where we were supposed to be lurking in deep water.

I got the bridge personnel rapidly below, shut the conning tower hatch, vented the main ballast tanks and the submarine sank, noiseless and still, on to the sandy sea bottom. The hull was concealed but the periscope standards stood out like a sore thumb.

Down below all was quiet. Men were motionless, breathing deeply. As the fast-moving vessel came closer, we could hear the roar of her propellers and the pings of her echo detector.

I told myself that the enemy would not distinguish our tophamper against the bluff and the tall reeds of the shoreline, that if he detected our hull with his echoes he would think that it was a nearby boulder and that, in any case, he believed that we lay further out and in his present path.

The throbbing propellers passed about half a mile to seaward and the vessel then slowed, turned and started a sophisticated search away from us, always increasing the length of his passes along our probable retreat line.

I then had time to consider MacRae and the canoe. I knew that he would have the sense to hug the side of the bluff. After some thirty minutes the sound of our foe diminished. I raised a periscope for a cautious look round, of limited value in the starlight, then blew out the ballast tanks to resurface for a hurried reembarkment of our doughty commando, who arrived on board, apparently unperturbed. The foredeck party collapsed the canoe and all got rapidly below. Before the hatch closed, I heard MacRae describe, in expletive Doric, what he thought of the cowboys ashore; and cowboys they were, lacking a concerted plan with the destroyer: without this plan, they had alerted me with their futile fire and neglected to camp out or post a watcher on the bluff, preferring the relative comfort of the fort. Well, bless them, the Italians did not have their hearts in Mussolini's war.

I beat a hasty retreat along the reciprocal line of our approach in case someone got up on top of the bluff. The destroyer was now too far to seaward to threaten us.

During the return to Port Said, I was free to attack the enemy but no targets presented themselves. This was the calm before a storm. I had time for introspective speculation.

Luigi was either a traitor to be welcomed ashore by the enemy, or he had been betrayed by an axis spy in our camp or by some indiscretion; in which case he was doubtless tortured or killed.

I felt scant trouble about his fate. I remembered again that he had been a friend of Simon, probably his lover, and that he was well known to Lee. I recalled Simon's warning of communists within the Command structure. On the one hand, the Communist Empire was still ranged against us, on the other, I remembered that in the 1914 war the Monarchist German Empire had inserted Lenin as a virus to destroy Russia from within, to wither the Russian armies and people's will to resist. Was Luigi a traitor, a dupe or a virus? And, God Almighty, what had been his relation with Lee? They had been in earnest conversation at that fateful party in Hong Kong, which preceded the attack on Lee in Wanchai. There were too many unknowns; it was like opening Pandora's box.

During our return passage, on April, 6th 1941, I received a signal containing the information that the axis powers had invaded Yugoslavia: I wondered if Luigi was with them.

On return to harbour, I submitted a factual and succinct report of the recent operation. I made no mention of the fact that I had met Luigi in the past, although this cost me considerable, inner moral conflict. I made no squeaky complaints about our narrow escape nor emphasised how I had achieved it. I suspected that the whole thing would be swept under the carpet and, for all I cared, it could stay there.

The submarine was well repaired in Port Said, well enough for a peaceful passage at slow speed. I sat up on the bridge conning the ship down the Suez Canal. The pilot was happy to leave it to me.

As we watched a train of camels, stark against the cloudless sky, a seaman passed up a decoded radio signal message. June, 22nd 1941, Hitler had turned on his ally and launched Operation Barbarossa, the invasion of the huge Russian Empire. I felt relief that we now had five million bayonets pointing at someone else, and some curiosity about Luigi's present attachment.

The unwarlike onward passage was a lapse into unreality. Down the Red Sea and across the Indian Ocean; calling at Aden and Colombo was a throwback to the British Raj, their cabins booked on the shady side Port Out and Starboard Home – POSH. It felt posh not to be harried by well-armed foes determined to kill.

We moved across a huge expanse of undisputed ocean, the sun shone, the look-outs bronzed and flying fish crash-landed on the saddle tanks to make me a nice fish breakfast. I enjoyed the ability to slip into neutral.

Chapter Twenty-One

An Empire Falls

So we came at our last gasp, to the tree-lined Johore Strait on the east side of Singapore Island leading to the naval base which faced the Malayan jungle. The fortifications were on the other side of the Island facing to seaward; huge shoremounted fifteen inch turreted guntowers along the steep. The main fleet was ten thousand miles away.

Some time after we had settled into our shore quarters, a naval staff car drove up to the door of my hutted office. It was Tom. He had been given treatment for his illness, some new brand of pills. He had a hectic flush and coughed. I realised that we must, on no account, go on any sort of booze-up and we spent our time swimming in the Tanglin Club freshwater pool, playing golf and eating quiet dinners in Chinese and Indian restaurants in the city. He had total use of the car and his naval chauffeur was happy to wait up.

We chatted ourselves up-to-date but he divulged nothing about his top-secret mission.

One important piece of information he let drop "Some day there may be a submarine base established here and possibly an operational submarine will arrive." He paused to let this sink in and continued, "I have the feeling that your boat is going to vegetate here, Bob. Make sure that you and your crew have an escape route and remember to forget that I told you this."

One day Tom was part of the scene, my link with the past; the next day, without warning, he was gone.

I took heed from his physical condition and mapped out a life for myself. I would not go to seed in the bars, clubs and pubs nor in the dance halls and whore-houses. I would rebuild my health by playing golf and swimming, for which there was pleasant opportunity, and I kept, by and large, to this resolve with enough lapses to make life tolerable.

I had lapsed one evening; it was in the Raffles or, perhaps, in a more lowlife place like "The New World", where there were taxi dancers. I was sitting at a table with a pretty blonde girl, the wife of a planter who was away up country. I was playing it cool not wanting to start a serious affair, the floor was crowded with dancers, a catchy out-of-date tune in the background.

Suddenly, there she was, or a figment of my disordered imagination – Lee dancing with a well-dressed, handsome Chinese. They were chatting, animated, he dancing superbly, she with the same style as she had riding her pony, a poetry of motion. They turned; I could not be mistaken. My companion looked startled. "Bob are you ill?" My colour must have drained.

"No," I said, "I have just seen a ghost." I started up, then sat back. Had Lee seen me? The dancing couple disappeared into the crowded throng. I sat with the girl. I was now so distant that she made moves to go – I could not relate to anyone else. She went. I sat alone for a few minutes and then made an exploratory tour of the dance floor tables and bar. There was no sign of Lee or her partner. Had I conjured up her image, which was always in the back of my mind? There was no way I could follow her trail, I must have had suspicions about her activities in the light of what I had heard about her history but I thrust them away into limbo.

Not long after this, the Japanese fleet attacked Pearl Harbour. The casualties had not been revealed officially but I met the Dutch pilot of a Catalina flying boat who came in from Hawaii. After a few gins he said:

"Eight American battleships are lying on the bottom."

I immediately recalled Tom's warning and made some contingency plans in my mind. I realised, in an almost extrasensory way, that Tom knew in his heart that Singapore was indefensible, that no main fleet could sail to its succour, that the main fleet was in any case obsolete. If we had, for instance, a fleet of large, fast, ocean-going submarines, well and good. We had some excellent, small, slow, well-armed, close-in-warfare boats, which someone described as mobile mines, and they were heavily engaged in the Mediterranean. What was needed was a lot of submersible torpedo boats.

I had a surge of memory of a voyeur's eyrie, in a brothel in Hong Kong, with a terrified prostitute lying beside me, a Japanese Admiral in the room below.

"Do not wake the American sleeping giant, do not confront."

Well they had done just that. I knew that the US Navy were building a fleet of fast, wide-ranging submersible torpedo boats: we were no longer alone at sea.

There was nothing I could presently do except keep calm and continue to have a lifestyle which, I hoped, abated the threat of disease which had attacked, besides Tom, two more of my surviving flotilla mates.

If the enemy could not destroy you in the killing-grounds, he could leave you with a slow death: the lung failure consequent to all those hours of trying to extract the oxygen as it vanished from the surrounding atmosphere. Reliving in my mind's eye the summer of 1940, those endless days without nights, I thought, "No one will ever understand what it was like." I walked the immaculate turf of the golf course. Overhead sounded an angry buzz from a superannuated biplane fighter aircraft, a Gloucester Gladiator, now our only defence and shield.

So, here I was, thousands of miles from home, no proper professional life, the so-called refit could go on without me, no sex life, no clear idea of the future, above all, no idea of what had happened to Lee or if I had really seen her. Had I imagined her? Was I trying to believe this against the fearful suspicions which were crowding into my conscious mind?

It was then that the Japanese army landed on the Malay Peninsula at Khota Baru. For me and my compatriots ensued a humiliating, short-lived but far reaching facet of history. The trouble was I found myself at the sharp end without a weapon.

The smell of defeat in the air was epitomised by the stink of unburied corpses trapped in the rubble of bombed buildings. A hastily landed Japanese army, inferior to the garrison in numbers, was pushing our forces southward through the jungle at the rate of ten miles per day. Great wedges of enemy bombers cruised unopposed overhead. Two capital ships, which had come to our rescue, were on the sea-bed.

The dockyard, where my submarine lay refitting in dry-dock on the north side of the island, facing the narrow, defenceless strait which the Japanese were approaching, was coming to a halt. I contemplated hijacking some small craft to escape with my crew but my initiative stultified. However, I managed to locate and embark the explosive depth-charge, which we habitually carried, as a last desperate measure of self-immolation to avoid the capture of the boat.

Chapter Twenty-Two

The Sun Rises

After the accommodation block had been flattened by a stray bomb, the officers were housed in an adjacent building, which consisted of an agglomeration of matsheds. There were no fans and the night was oppressively hot.

I slept naked under a sheet, restless at first, on account of the insect life.

I then slept unusually soundly, pleasantly tired, after playing golf while aircraft, mostly unfriendly, buzzed overhead.

I was awakened by a Malay mess steward shining a torch in my eyes and shaking my shoulder, "Captain wake, Captain wake."

I jumped out of bed thinking I was at sea and being called to the bridge: then, realising where I was, put on my sarong which hung over a chair beside my bed. The Malay lit an oil lamp and I saw that there was another man in the room: a European in civilian clothes; he had the withdrawn expression of those who exert power behind the scene, dark, of medium height and build. He radiated authority. He said, "I can't give you my name or rank, you may know me as Clive. I have here orders for you of the utmost urgency and secrecy. You are to carry them out without question. You are to leave here; you have an hour to make your arrangements." The strange visitor then produced the written orders, with the stamp of high rank and the highest precedence of secrecy.

"You are to proceed at once by fast launch to rendezvous with a Catalina flying boat... in position... and proceed then to Colombo, Ceylon, for further orders, having turned over your command to your First Lieutenant.

I was accustomed to sudden, unpredictable moves in war, but this was the winner in its class.

I told the visitor that my First Lieutenant was asleep in the matshed and suggested he wait in my room while I turned over my command. I woke Bill Frazer, and when he got to his senses, I gave him the works. "I have to go away now, don't ask why or where. You are to take command and this is what you must do. This place is bound to fall, but don't tell anyone I said so. I know that a British operational submarine is to come here very soon. When she arrives, consult no one but get the commanding officer to take the remnants of the crew away when he finally leaves: blow up the submarine in the dry dock with the depth charge we kept to immolate ourselves in case of capture; everyone will think it's a bomb. I leave the details to you. I suggest you approach the submarine's first lieutenant on the old boy frequency and get him to work on the skipper. It will make a crush in the boat but there are so few of us left that it is possible. Submariners look after their own."

He took all this in, muffled his surprise and said, "Can do, sir, no wanchee makee die, best of luck and happy landings."

Back in my room, I stuffed my few clothes and possessions into a battered suitcase and an old Hong Kong wicker basket, took up my hooded torch and followed the mysterious visitor down to the jetty where the appointed launch was waiting. She had a naval crew and an officer with navigational equipment. From the speed with which we were making down the main channel to the south of Singapore Island, I realised that they were familiar with the waterway; then, once clear of the channel, we roared off towards an offshore island anchorage. I feared that our wake would draw some prowling Jap aircraft and, indeed, wondered if Japanese surface ships were already in our vicinity. Lying to a mooring in the small bay was a US Navy, long, range Catalina flying boat, her swanlike fuselage clean-cut in the starlight. We launched a small collapsible dinghy and transferred to the flying boat, my silent civilian companion carrying a locked holder containing the orders chained to his wrist. I thought to myself, "He is doing this for a film".

As we boarded, dawn was breaking; the engines sprang to life, we slipped the moorings and roared up into the sky.

I thought we would fly up the Malacca Straits and over the mountains of Sumatra but the pilot did not want to gain height, which he thought would give us publicity, and turned south flying low through the Sunda Strait between Java and Sumatra, beside the Island of Krakatoa, where took place in 1883 the greatest explosion in history; a volcanic eruption which blew the island in half. The slice could be clearly seen and it also went below the sea for one hundred fathoms. We flew out into the Indian Ocean to escape from the war and then headed for Ceylon.

The sun rose vertically from behind the mountains of Sumatra, which faded into a limitless, blue ocean. As we gained height I fell asleep in my seat.

The sun was well up when I was woken by a US Naval rating serving me a mug of excellent coffee. "We picked it up in Java," he explained, and then followed breakfast of eggs and bacon. At this point we were joined by another man in civilian clothes, emerging from the cockpit. He was large, well-built, the epitome of strength, health and aggression. His strong features bore the mark of ruthlessness. I took an instant dislike to him. Clive introduced him to me as Peter and indicated that we should be working closely together in Ceylon. I knew better than to enquire about his background. "What," I wondered, "were they up to, and why was I being evacuated from Singapore when there were many more important and valuable people who would not get away?" I could not resist a feeling of relief at my certain escape, though I had planned to exit in the submarine, which I felt would almost certainly rescue my crew. For all the other 90,000 strong garrison there was nothing I could do. The plane droned on over the blue sea; far away to our right and then fading astern, a ruthless, well-trained enemy was closing in on Singapore. I was given some old copies of Readers' Digest to riffle through. I thought it would have been preferable to have prepared myself for what was to come but nothing was said by reticent Clive or taciturn Peter. The day passed pleasantly enough, the sun shot overhead with tropical abruptness and its setting mirrored the sunset of the Empire. The night struck cold and I was lent a warm jacket and blanket, dozing fitfully or staring out at the stars. The lovely mountains of Ceylon showed up in the starlight and we alighted on the sea just outside Colombo Harbour and transferred to a waiting RAF launch. I was taken to my quarters, a comfortable room in the Great Eastern Hotel, in Colombo, and told by Clive to take a day to rest. "Tomorrow," he said, "you will see Commander The Earl of Mountbriach."

"Good God," I said, "what is Simon to do with all this?"

Clive looked reproving. Then he and Peter vanished, the latter moving, I noticed, with cat-like agility; a large cat – perhaps a tiger.

I had twenty-four hours to myself, rest, cleanliness, good meals and introspection, trying to slough off the horror of Singapore, to guess what Clive, Peter and Simon were up to. I knew Simon had been working for Naval Intelligence, whose higher secrets were hidden from most junior officers. However, submarine Commanding Officers had, by nature of their work with clandestine operations and secret knowledge of the enemy's movements, frequent insight into matters far above their station; but nothing I could have imagined prepared me for what next transpired.

As I finished breakfast, a Sinhalese major-domo whispered in my ear, "Officer to see you, sir, in your room."

Simon looked well but strained. Our old warm feelings of friendship flooded back, forged in early youth it transcended our differences, the fact that we were on opposite sides of the sexual divide, the rift that had occurred during my affair with Caroline. We talked awhile of Tom Farr, now closely involved with Simon in secret intelligence work. Tom was no longer obviously destined for high rank. Simon said he, personally, intended to retire when war ended. Nothing significant would remain of his Irish estate but he hoped to carve a smallholding for himself out of the remnants; with him the title and family connection would die out. After an hour or so, I ordered coffee from the room service and Simon settled into his chair with the obvious intention of explaining his mission and my extraordinary flight from disaster.

The clear light from the window fell on his face whereon premature lines showed the burden which he carried. "First, Bob, I will give you the background. It is all about Lee O'Connor." Simon paused; apart from my astonishment at this disclosure I was struck by an emotional thunderbolt. Lee, the only woman I had ever loved, almost certainly the only one whom I ever would love, was fighting on the other side, always had been. A whole train of unconnected events began to couple up. Simon continued:

"Her father was an Irish Colonel in the British Army during the 1914 War. Many Irishmen joined up under the leadership of Redmond, the Irish nationalist, who made, I think, the mistake of not standing out for the granting of Irish Independence at the time. A terrible sourness erupted when the British shot the leaders of the abortive 1916 rebellion. This sourness was felt by Red O'Connor. He was posted as missing believed killed; actually he had deserted."

I kept my own counsel, and hoped that my expression did not betray the fact that I already knew most of this.

"Red went to Belfast and shipped out as a stoker in a coal burning ship, bound for Australia, where he had friends who concealed him and enabled him to join the small community of schooners trading among the Pacific Islands. He left a daughter in Ireland, illegitimate and thought to be half-Chinese. She, Lee, was actually the grand-daughter of a Japanese nobleman who became an Admiral. She was brought up, in the west of Ireland, by an eccentric cousin, Roderick O'Connor. Roderick had her raised in a family of healthy peasants and saw that she was well educated. Red made his way to Japan. The old admiral, Lee's grandfather, was long dead; his nephew, also an admiral, was living. Red managed to contact him. I can't think why Red was not killed for dishonouring the family; probably because it appeared that he might be useful to them in a way which will now become apparent as I move into the foreground. Meanwhile, let's have some more coffee."

I rang for room service and, feeling that Simon was in a mood and position to reveal anything which had a bearing on this, I decided to probe further;

"Simon, I thought that you were a fervent Irish Nationalist?"

He rose and stood for a moment looking out towards the harbour. "If you are born and brought up in a country where your ancestors have lived since the middle ages, how can you fail to be part of that land? Nonetheless, I was never a separatist. I felt that Ireland could exist happily within the Empire, if she had her own parliament."

"And Lee?"

"The priest who educated Lee was in touch with the most violently inclined Nationalists."

I had taken in what little was added to my own knowledge of the story. The old admiral had not launched an expedition to rescue his daughter because he had died. The rest of the family had not then involved themselves. The little girl grew up on the western seaboard of Europe; healthy, handsome, very well-educated, very intelligent and imbued with dislike of the British and their Empire. Roderick must have taken her back into his own home and introduced her to the grand world and enjoined her to keep her own counsel. But still I was not prepared for what followed, when fresh, hot coffee arrived and Simon resumed.

"Lee was and is a Japanese spy. Not one of those small-time jokers, who find out the secrets of the fort or seduce some diplomat, but a top-level agent. She moved in the highest academic and social circles which interface with the corridors of power. Her role was to feel the pulse and political will of nations."

Simon paused and must have seen my expression change: he took a draught of coffee and continued.

"Far more important and dangerous is the fact that, as well as working for the High Command, she was part of a well-knit political and military group of Germans and Japanese, who jointly evolved a combined Grand Strategy, which was likely to have been far more effective than that which has already been deployed and, indeed, could still be extremely dangerous if the enemies' plans were to sway back into their control. Fortunately, the high policy makers in both countries moved away from this. There was always opposition and both countries appear to fall short of full co-operation and prefer to regard each other as friendly enemies rather than true allies. This attitude stems from their systems and pride.

Here is the broad plan and its essence lay in what not to do. The principles of this were: for Germany – do not oppose Russia on a front broader than between Odessa and East Prussia, about five hundred miles. Note, if you go further east, the front soon nearly doubles in length. Above all, do not attack north of the Pripet Marshes. Drive east, therefore, with huge concentration through the Ukraine and Caucasus, a southern punch into the Tigris and Euphrates valleys and the oil-fields and the Persian Gulf and on to Aden, alternatively through Turkey, Syria and Palestine.

For the Japanese: again the do nots: do not oppose the USA, wear olive branches and appear to withdraw from the China adventure. The threat of the US fleet from the Philippines on the flank of the South China Sea is contained by the Japanese Empire on the flank of the route from Hawaii to the Philippines.

Do not start a land drive into Burma and India, but forge a ring of steel around them. Drive for Singapore, Ceylon, Aden, the Persian Gulf. The British have no modern taskforce to command the Indian Ocean. The powerful people opposed to these policies appear to have won the day but two terrible dangers exist. An attack on Ceylon is thought to be imminent and" he paused, "Lee is in Ceylon."

I reacted with disbelief. "Good God, is she having dinner with the Governor?"

"No, she is in the jungle working with a local dissident group and this is where you come in."

I reacted with fervour, "So how did she get here and what is her backup in the jungle? And for God's sake, Simon, you must have known something of her activities before war broke out."

Simon stirred uneasily, "Of course I knew much about her from our family connections but, Bob, don't think that for one moment my Irishness has sapped my loyalty to what we are fighting for. I think that the English behaved with amazing stupidity towards Ireland and also towards Japan but, as far as I am concerned, it is the Royal Navy against some very nasty aggressors." He smiled ruefully. "I guess, Bob, with you it is narrower loyalty – The Submarine Service against the rest." He reverted to the main theme, picking up where I had interrupted him.

"The bond between Ceylon and Japan is Buddhism. The Sinhalese are Buddhists. There is a considerable amount of Buddhism in Japan, though of a very different nature, say like Protestants and Catholics – nonetheless, a link was forged.

Lee was probably landed by a fishing boat to which she had been transferred from a Japanese submarine. The Buddhist link is tenuous and likely to break – The Commander-in-Chief went into the jungle and personally thanked some Buddhist monks, who had rescued and cared for the pilot of one of our planes, which had crash-landed nearby, a simple act of humanism."

I was torn by an agony of retrospect. "My God, with her wonderful spirit and humour, religion and philosophy, how can she have sided with these monsters?"

Simon considered for a moment, drank more coffee. "Her religion is real and sincere but, if you are a top agent, you do not go around with 'I spy' written on your shirt. I think her philosophy was based on a huge stable Asiatic Empire. Ghengis Khan achieved that after ferocious, cruel wars. The British Empire was not stabilised without slaughter. Stability finally brings peace and security – until the Empire falls. The Irish extreme nationalists reached out to Philip of Spain, Napoleon, The Kaiser, Hitler – anyone who would get the

English off their backs. Conversely, the Northern Protestants don't like the English, they just hate the Catholics more, and remember that Carson, the leader of Ulster's Secessionists, dickered with the Kaiser, hoping that if Germany were to win the war, they might keep a northern Irish Protestant enclave." A fraught silence ensued.

Simon continued, "We have penetrated the local group. Lee appears to be wavering. She has suffered years of frustration. The policies formulated by her uncle and a high-up German staff officer were negated. At one time the opposition appeared to have taken out a contract on her life. We think that she is now turned. You are the only person in the world to whom she extended any lasting friendship and she will almost certainly refuse to emerge from the jungle unless you are present.

You are to go up to Nuwara Eliya, a pleasant hill station about five thousand feet above sea-level. Stay in the club, amuse yourself playing golf or whatever. Peter will also be staying but you are not to approach one another until he gives the word. Peter is an extremely efficient agent, though, personally, he is not my cup of tea. All your expenses will be met, do your shopping today and a car will take you into the mountains tomorrow."

I pondered, the meeting in Ethel's brothel had not been an absurd charade. The German, although an obsessive brothel creeper, had been in the core of a far-seeing group of world-power-seeking strategists, the other, a Japanese Admiral, probably Lee's uncle. The agent described had been assumed by the German to be male; the Japanese never disclosed the real gender. The top agent was Lee. I rejoined,

"So what then happened to Red O'Connor? How did he influence these events?"

"That was an old trail and hard to follow. He disappeared into the tough, hard-drinking life of a Pacific trader, sailing his schooner round the islands. Magnetically drawn towards Japan, Red, like many Irishmen of his class, had his loyalty split between Ireland as a separate entity and the British Empire.

Whatever philosophical searching went on in his mind during this period fused his loyalty into a violently intense Irish nationalism.

He sailed north and, from one of the Japanese offshore islands, he contacted Lee's maternal family, particularly her uncle, a naval officer destined for high rank, embittered by the Naval Treaty of

1921, which relegated Japan to inferiority, and devoted to Japanese expansion.

Red was tidied up, indoctrinated, disguised – he was still unwilling to have the story of his desertion betrayed – and transported to Ireland.

He seems to have failed to strike up a relationship with his daughter, a healthy, lovely, very bright child. She did not know him... "

I broke in, "What about love?"

Simon, clearly irritated by the interruption, said, "Fanaticism kills love", and continued, unimpeded, "Red did two vitally important things. He converted his cousin, Rory, an archetypal Celtic-Twilight eccentric romantic into a new mould, a supporter of a violent struggle for a united Ireland; and he enlisted a priest of immense intelligence and fiery militancy to educate Lee under Rory's aegis. Further, he gave the priest the signs for a pathway to Japan and to her maternal family."

"What happened to Red in the end?" I could not forebear from asking that banal question. Simon paused, diverted from his main theme.

"He did not long outlive his usefulness to his cause; broke his neck schooling a young horse over jumps; must have been out of practice and too old. History might have been different had he done this a bit earlier. Fate hangs on chances."

I made a desperate move. "Were you in love with Lee?"

Simon turned to me a frank expression, as though a catharsis had taken place; his gaze was level and devoid of embarrassment and hostility.

"Yes, and with Caroline. As well as being a homosexual, I must have had a cousin complex: or was it that I happened to have two extremely attractive cousins? Neither of them loved me."

I was struck by an old guilt.

"But, for God's sake, Simon, what happened to Caroline?" Simon did not hesitate. He had a bizarre tale to tell.

"Caroline was a strong girl; she was easily cured of her illness and had a healthy baby. The baby was adopted by a childless French couple, refugees, who had escaped across the English Channel in a Breton fishing boat. Caroline joined the Poor Clares."

"Poor what!" I exclaimed.

"They are an enclosed order of Catholic nuns. Personally and totally shut off from the world, they offer up continuous prayer. They have a window to those in trouble, who can unload their problems to a link who sits behind a screen. They were founded at Assisi in... "

"That's enough," I broke in, "I just hope that she found peace. I had a frightful hang-up. I couldn't love her, just used her. Well, we had fun. I just can't picture her in a permanent retreat." Then I remembered her affection for Catholic Ireland.

Having gone so far, I wanted to dig deeper into Simon's emotional morass to settle an appalling doubt, which I had previously resolved by relegating it to that limbo of the mind where dwell those shadowy figures which we are unwilling to face; the guilts of ourselves or our friends.

"Simon," I hesitated. "You remember that chap in Hong Kong, Luigi was it?" I looked at the floor.

Simon heaved out of the depth of his armchair into an erect sit-up. I sensed that he had, perhaps like most of us, a mental carpet under which intolerable past situations could be swept.

"Luigi was the love of my life." He shook his head as though to clear it and continued, "It was a one-off thing. There can never be another such."

He paused, long enough for me to register the thought that I was in a similar situation.

"He was an idealistic communist, had embraced communism with the fervour with which he had previously held to the Italian Catholicism of his childhood. His father, a doctor, born a Serb, was a naturalised Italian. Slowly but surely, the Communist Manipulators wove him into their structure. To cut a very long story short, in the early stages of the war he was in the grey area when Stalin was standing behind Hitler. At that time, our people, who were communistic were regarded as non-prosecutable traitors.

Another of my friends, who fought against Franco in Spain, was given the hospitality of an officers' mess but not allowed to join our armed forces. Yes, it really happened (in response to my raised eyebrows). There were a lot of split mentalities around; intelligence work is a litany of deceit.

One of our high-ups in Cairo was a Communist. Luigi was his side-kick. There were spiders' webs reaching out from them to people in the axis camp engaged in the supply of oil and grain from

Russia. Also, with their people who thought that the Communists in Yugoslavia could be played off against Mihailovitch and the Royalists. So, in this tangled web, your submarine got shopped."

Simon relaxed, sat back in his chair, cradled his coffee cup in both hands and continued:

"Bob, rest your mind, my desk was in London, totally separate from Cairo. I've not seen Luigi since I left Hong Kong. Banish any dark thoughts which you may harbour."

I banished them.

After Simon had left, I ordered a third replenishment of coffee and sat ruminating, putting together the jigsaw puzzle, of which I had been slowly becoming half aware over a long period of time. Simon, his father and Caroline, all related to Lee, had fed me information, disconnected at the time but which now made a clear picture. Strong emotions made it impossible for me to coalesce my feelings into firm outlines. When I thought of Lee all that emerged was abiding love.

I switched my thoughts towards the shipwreck of the huge British Empire, which was being caused not so much by the efficiency of the Teutonic war machine as by bad navigation around the rocks; neglected Ireland to which no positive thought had ever been given, and the Rising Sun, once encouraged as a counterbalance to Russian expansion and then brushed off into third place as a naval also-ran; the dangerous powder keg of hurt pride and fanaticism.

Lee, the embodiment of all this, was the most dangerous of all. The half-covered shoal. Red O'Connor must have been used to co-opt her into the top ring of enemy intelligence. The bright star of academic and social life in the western world had found her fulfilment in the East.

Of course I had been assailed by deep-down suspicions, when I heard the news of Lee's concealed Japanese ancestry and of her father having deserted from the battlefield in 1916: but these suspicions had been thrust into the background, mostly by my blinding love for Lee and, possibly, by the stress of my crumbling affair with Caroline and the always immediate toils of a very sticky war.

I turned over in my mind the sequence of outstanding events. Lee had always turned up at the key points along the storm path; in Hong Kong, when the Japanese were dismantling China, in Alexandria, during the Italian conquest of Ethiopia, the forerunner to our loss of maritime control of the Mediterranean, in Singapore before its fall and now in Ceylon. I wondered bitterly if she had been in Scotland in 1931, when the Home Fleet mutinied at Invergordon. The Japanese had walked into Manchuria ten days later. They must have known that the Royal Navy, the only force which could restrain them, was in no shape to do so.

I had a clear memory; Lee's cry in the farmhouse during the typhoon was "Kamikaze", which meant "The Divine Wind". The violent attack in Wanchai must have been set up by those opposed to the broad strategy of a Southern punch link up. The cry of the fleeing-injured assailant was "Ninja!" – the underground, criminal dispossessed, samurai; was he meant to kill or warn?

All this was subordinate to the present frightful threats to the cause, for which we had fought so desperately, to which I was fiercely loyal. How much, I wondered, had Simon known or guessed in the past? What shadowy shift had gone on in his mind? Above all, what was I to do now? How ought I to react, how would I react in reality?

I idled gloriously in The Nuwara Eliya Club, striking up brief friendships with elderly tea-planters and service people on leave and played a lot of golf and tennis. I noticed that golf and tennis balls fly better in thin air at high altitude. Peter remained in a shadowy background; he came and went but we never acknowledged one another. While this sybaritic existence continued, I heard the catastrophic news from the outside world. Singapore fell, Burma was threatened and an allied naval squadron destroyed in the Java Sea. The Dutch East Indies fell, an obsolete British Fleet assembled in Colombo and left hurriedly. Then, on April 5th, Easter Day, came the attack on Colombo and operations, by a powerful, modern Japanese taskforce, sweeping the Bay of Bengal and sinking two of our cruisers, an aircraft carrier and about 100,000 tons of merchant shipping. I felt numb from the bombardment of news of disaster creeping ever closer.

Two days after the attack, Peter came to my room. "We start at midnight with lanterns for the top of Mount Pedrotogaila." Mount Pedro, (about 7,000 feet), rose above and dominated the Nuwara Eliya plateau. I had climbed it long ago. The summit, reached by an easy scramble up a jungle track, gave an intensely rewarding view over the middle and low country of Ceylon, the paradise isle. "What am I supposed to do?" I asked Peter. It seemed absurd to use his Christian name, even if it was not his true one.

"Act as judgement says is proper," he replied. I wondered why he seemed to dislike me and then realised that this was reciprocal. He was geared more for action than for small talk.

I went to bed early and slept soundly, until wakened by a servant with a cup of tea, sometime after midnight. I put on a bush shirt and shorts and carried a sweater for the top which I knew would be cold. Peter was waiting at the door and carried two lanterns and a rifle.

Irritation got the better of me and I remarked crossly to Peter:

"For God's sake, why go to the trouble of a rendezvous at the top of the highest mountain in the island?"

Peter assumed the air of an indulgent parent instructing a child.

"If you are to call an agent out of thousands of square miles of jungle, you can't meet at the third Baobab tree on the left. Mount Pedro dominates the entire jungle area, you can't miss it."

I realised with no little dismay that I was live bait; that Peter was armed in case Lee appeared with an armed escort. I wondered, but forbore to ask, why I was not armed. I suppose that Peter considered that a sailor would be useless in a fire fight. I had not informed him that I was a crack shot, nor would I.

I was fit from all the exercise I had been taking and Peter, I imagined, was always fit. We made light of the ascent. As we neared the summit, there was a clear light from the blazing stars and a half moon and we left our lanterns beside the track. We got to the top and I had time to take in the awakening scene, when Lee appeared out of a nearby thicket. She looked thinner and travel-worn but, otherwise, just as she had been on Ma-on-Shan when the tiger died. Peter, beside me, raised his rifle and pointed at her. I knocked it upwards and the bullet whistled into the air.

Lee shot him through the heart with a handgun. As he crumpled and fell, Lee dropped her pistol and came towards me and into my arms. Behind her the sun shot up into the sky.

Chapter Twenty-Three

And Sets

The word love is hackneyed by the diversity of its meanings. The Ancient Greeks used about six variations; the English Dictionary has many explanations. Sex was first described to me as "dirty", an admonitory deterrent no doubt: well it does go on around the excretory organs and childbirth is a messy operation.

Swans are almost always faithfully monogamous, humans much less so. It is certain that, if you fall in love with someone because of their particular qualities, there are, at the same time, a vast number of people scattered around the globe who possess those qualities in a greater degree.

My love for Lee was, at the start, fired by Lee's outstanding beauty and brightness, but this situation had soon deepened into an overwhelming swan-like empathy, which could have bestrode a loss of looks by some accident or even a deterioration of bright-mindedness.

Now she was in my arms. I had never before touched her, not even with a social kiss or handshake. She said, "It's all over, we have lost. They won't attack Ceylon. There will be stupid, steamroller attacks on all fronts, which are bound to fail. My war is over and it has failed." Then she said, "Bob, I love you. I always have done."

A surge of joy rushed up from my solar plexus, through my chest and brain with a fullness that excluded thought and speech. I stood, holding her.

Dawn had just broken on top of the highest peak in the loveliest island in the world. I was cut off from those surroundings and from the dead man close by, nor did any idea of sex enter my mind. It happened naturally, seemingly without volition. My usual obsession with orgasm was resolved into a glorious sunburst. I had come home after a very long voyage. I stroked her lovingly, murmuring, "For ever, it's for ever." But the home was burning down, the world was coming to an end for after a while Lee rose and moved away from me, put on her clothes and faced towards the rising sun.

Then she knelt down. I saw that she had a knife in her hand. She let out a wild cry "Seppukku", plunging the knife into the artery on the left side of her neck. Her life-blood jetted out and she fell, dying quickly. There was nothing I could do, nor I think anything I could have done.

I was alone with the dead, emotionally too stricken to care about what would happen next.

I lifted Lee and, putting her over my shoulders in a fireman's lift, started back down the trail. Blood, whose pulsing had ceased, ran down my leg. Two mighty empires were falling, a dead man lay on the mountain with my guilt upon him. I cared for none of these things nor what might become of me. I carried my world on my shoulder. I shed no tears. Words are inadequate to describe such grief and loneliness; a huge, empty space. Wolves howling around a dark whirlpool.